APRIL TWILIGHTS (1903)

April Twilights (1903)

Revised Edition

Poems by
WILLA CATHER

Edited with an introduction by
BERNICE SLOTE

UNIVERSITY OF NEBRASKA PRESS
LINCOLN AND LONDON

The poems are reprinted from the 1903 edition of *April Twilights*, published in Boston by Richard G. Badger at the Gorham Press. Typographical and orthographical emendations are listed by the editor in the notes beginning on page 53. *April Twilights (1903)* first appeared in 1962 in cloth and paper editions; there was a second printing of the paper edition in 1964. The revised edition was first published in 1968 in cloth only, was reprinted in paper in 1976, and was subsequently reprinted in cloth in 1981.

Library of Congress Cataloging in Publication Data

Cather, Willa Sibert, 1873–1947.
   April twilights (1903)

   "A Bison book."
   Bibliography: p.
   I. Title.
PS3505.A87A8   1976   811'.5'2   76–14216
ISBN 0–8032–0011–0 (cl.)
ISBN 0–8032–5851–8 (pbk.)

Manufactured in the United States of America

Preface to the Revised Edition

✳

In 1962, the reissue of the 1903 version of *April Twilights* was the beginning of a University of Nebraska Press project to collect the previously unavailable early writings of Willa Cather. Poetry (and especially some of the 1903 volume) was of course incidental to Willa Cather's major accomplishments; but some things, though not at the center of one's creative interests, may at the same time account for a great deal that goes on elsewhere. As Elizabeth Shepley Sergeant said in *Willa Cather: A Memoir*, "A good case could be made for the reissue of *April Twilights*, if only because Willa herself had the poet's response to life, including the typical sense of the lyric poet that youth and the emotions of youth, because of their great intensity and simplicity, surpass all other emotions" (pp. 182–183). Miss Sergeant was speaking then of the publication of *April Twilights and Other Poems* in 1923—a collection which was only in part a reissue of the 1903 volume—but her statement holds even more logically for Willa Cather's first experiments in verse. Anyone who is interested in her major fiction and its interpretation will find the 1903 *April Twilights* wholly relevant.

This new edition of *April Twilights* (*1903*), with a revised and amplified introduction and checklist, attests to the authentic place these minor works have in Willa Cather's whole career. For although the original study I began with *April Twilights* has led me to a very great amount of new material and information about Willa Cather, I find that nothing of the basic study of relationships first presented in "Willa Cather and Her First Book" needs to be changed. If anything, every major point made in 1962 has instead been confirmed and strengthened. I have therefore revised the introductory essay only to incorporate more material on Willa Cather's ideas about poetry and her literary backgrounds before 1903, to amplify some statements, and to correct whatever might give a wrong idea of the facts or of my meaning. I have added some items to the checklist of Willa Cather's published poetry and have included an Appendix of certain of her early verses that seem related to her "literary biography."

The reissue of *April Twilights* in 1962 has had some unexpected results. Though it is certainly not a usual experience, I have learned of readers who liked the poems of 1903 better than what they had previously read of Willa Cather (often it was only the much-anthologized "Paul's Case" they had studied in school) and so were led with delight to the novels. One friend has told me that as he was growing up he knew of Willa Cather only as the author of a poem which his mother often read to him. It was "'Grandmither, Think Not I Forget,'" which she had clipped from a magazine or newspaper and had kept with affection for years. To me, one of the great rewards of the 1962 edition of *April Twilights (1903)* was that it led both Elizabeth Shepley Sergeant and Mrs. George Seibel to write to me, and afterward give encouragement and help. The original study has also brought me to other materials that I hope will be useful in the understanding of Willa Cather's work. Some of the story of her own youth and early writing is in *The Kingdom of Art: Willa Cather's First Principles and Critical Statements, 1893–1896*, published in 1967 by the University of Nebraska Press.

I have also been increasingly convinced of something many others know well—that the more one goes into a subject, the more difficult it is to make flat and unequivocal statements; that truth is not only deep but complex, and almost never complete. In the end, it is only a close, personal reading of the works themselves that will bring a reader near to the writer's reality.

I am indebted to many sources: to Mildred R. Bennett and the Willa Cather Pioneer Memorial, Red Cloud, Nebraska, for the loan of materials including the announcement reproduced in this book; to John March, for special assistance in checking references; to the Cather family, for the loan of valuable materials; to the late Elsie Cather, to Norman Foerster, and to Mrs. George Seibel for personal reminiscences; to all on the staff of the Nebraska State Historical Society, and especially to particular help given by Dr. Donald F. Danker, archivist Douglas Bakken, Paul D. Riley, and Mrs. Opal Jacobsen and her colleagues in the newspaper room; to staff of the University of Nebraska Libraries, the Bennett Martin Public Library of Lincoln, the Carnegie Library of Pittsburgh, and the Newberry Library of Chicago for many courtesies.

Some of the research on the first edition of *April Twilights (1903)* was done as a part of a larger project for which I received a Frank H. Woods

Fellowship in the Humanities, 1960–1961, with related work continuing during a similar fellowship in 1967–1968. I am indeed grateful to the Woods Charitable Fund, Inc., for its active support of work in the humanities.

BERNICE SLOTE

University of Nebraska

Willa Cather and Her First Book

❖

This edition of Willa Cather's first book, her poems of *April Twilights* (1903), presents in full what has been an almost lost, certainly blurred, portion of the creative life of a great novelist. Her own selection and revision of poems to be reprinted in the 1923 volume, *April Twilights and Other Poems*, and later in the 1937 *April Twilights* of her collected works, must stand as her mature and final judgment about her art, and will be so respected. But the first book has its own value in the understanding of an extraordinary—and human—talent. For one thing, Willa Cather had buried nearly one-third of the poems of her early volume, and of the thirteen she rejected, eleven were never reprinted after 1903. Some of these poems have particular interest in the whole of Cather's writing; perhaps more than most artists she worked a single, intricate design in which elements changed names and language and form but always remained a part of the body. Nothing in her work is unrelated to the whole. In the poems (as in the first stories, some of which she also rejected), we find the early sketches, the first motifs, the suggested design of her major work. Willa Cather often said that she had absorbed all of her material before she was fifteen. One might also say that she had most of it written down—in some form—by 1903.

"I do not take myself seriously as a poet," said Willa Cather in 1925.[1] But by then she had found her way, and *April Twilights* had helped her find it. In the following pages, we can take a longer look at the chronology of Willa Cather as poet, the kind of poetry she wrote in the first *April Twilights*, and the relationship of that work to her whole design.

I

Willa Cather began in the great tradition: Her first published poem—in the University of Nebraska *Hesperian* for June, 1892—was on Shakespeare, the "sun born bard" whose power and mystery are beyond our

---

1. Quoted by Alice Hunt Bartlett in "The Dynamics of American Poetry—XI," *Poetry Review*, XVI (1925), 408.

reach, even as men of Ithaca could not bend Odysseus' bow of clanging silver. Above all our efforts,

the sun stands still in heaven,
Pierced there long centuries with a shaft of song.

"Shakespeare" was to be followed in other issues of campus publications by a poem on Columbus ("Upon the swift wings of thy dreams, a world / Fast followed and thou didst create the west") and several light variations on Horace and Anacreon.[2] She was a freshman at the university that spring of 1892, a girl just past eighteen, in the third movement of an odyssey that had progressed from Virginia, her birthplace, to the breaking of the great prairie in Nebraska near Red Cloud, where she had come with her family in 1883, and now to the larger imaginative world of books and creative vigor.

But even before the university—in the Red Cloud country where people of all nations joined like a patchwork quilt of customs and languages over the lands of the new West—Willa Cather had found the deep sources of poetry: the Bible, Shakespeare, and the classics. She absorbed the books in the Cather home—volumes of Campbell, Moore, Longfellow, Keats, Arnold, Poe; read Ben Jonson and Byron; learned of Emerson and transcendentalism from her Aunt Franc; and studied Latin and Greek with William Ducker, an Englishman well grounded in the classics who settled with his family in Red Cloud. They read Virgil, Ovid, Homer, and the odes of Anacreon.[3] Here were the forms and themes that determined her first conceptions of poetry. They led directly into what she studied more formally in the next years.

The courses Willa Cather took at the University of Nebraska from 1891 to her graduation in 1895 are significant enough in the shaping of her later work to justify some detail. Her records for the four years (which I have examined) show that she took English, Greek, Latin, French, German, and little else. The records give her course as "Philosophical" (or,

2. Complete references for all poems are in the Bibliography at the back of this book. For the texts of "Shakespeare," "Columbus," and a selection of other uncollected poems, see the Appendix.

3. The basic account of Willa Cather's Red Cloud experiences is Mildred R. Bennett, *The World of Willa Cather* (New edition with notes and index; Lincoln: University of Nebraska Press, 1961). A more complete presentation of the biographical material summarized in this introduction, and the texts of some of Willa Cather's journalistic writings, will be found in *The Kingdom of Art: Willa Cather's First Principles and Critical Statements, 1893–1896*, edited with a commentary and two essays by Bernice Slote (Lincoln: University of Nebraska Press, 1967). This volume will be cited hereafter as *KA*.

as it was in full—"Literary, English, Philosophical"), though she seems to have had a mixture of "Philosophical" and "Classical." The difference between the two groups was chiefly in languages, the Classical course requiring both Latin and Greek but no modern languages and science, and the Philosophical course requiring Latin, modern languages, and science. Willa Cather did elect to take some Greek courses that were primarily for the "Classicals"—Greek Lyric Poetry, for one. In her courses in language and literature, she had eighteen semesters of English, including two years of Shakespeare, a semester of Elizabethan dramatists, one year of Browning, and one year of other writers (Tennyson, Emerson, Hawthorne, Ruskin). The other courses in English included rhetoric, journalism, dramatization, and Anglo-Saxon literature. She had three years of Greek (Pindar, Homer, Herodotus, the dramatists), with an additional semester as an auditor; two years of Latin; one year of German; three semesters (plus one as auditor) of French (Daudet, Gautier, Balzac, Racine, Taine). In addition, she also had one year of history, one semester of philosophy, and freshman chemistry and mathematics.

Thus the pattern is clearly set: Shakespeare and the drama will loom large in her experience and interests; the adventure, mystery, and lyric tone of the Latin and Greek will stir her imagination; the more contemporary French and German writers will influence her style and her judgment of modern literature. And Browning? He would give the title of "'A Death in the Desert,'" and perhaps more. Many years later she told Norman Foerster (her friend and former student) that she believed Browning was popular because he always arrived at the old truths, but by a circuitous and fascinating route[4]—Like Henry James, it was the *way* he did it. As she sometimes quoted from Michelet, "The road is all."

But the courses were by no means all. There was Herbert Bates, one of her instructors, who wrote poetry and taught versification (though the records do not show that she took this course). *Songs of Exile* (1896), his first collection of poems, was written from the point of view of the homesick Easterner sojourning in the West. Poems by Bates often appeared in the *Hesperian*, on which Willa Cather was literary editor (1892–1893) and then managing editor (1893–1894). From the pages of the *Hesperian* come the shine of new things in the young prairie university, a current of real intellectual excitement—notes on art, music, and literature; even mention

4. Letter to Norman Foerster (Sept. 6, 1911), now in the possession of the University of Nebraska Libraries. Because of restrictions in Miss Cather's will, it may not be quoted.

of new writers like Whitman and Emily Dickinson. During her editorship, it seems, a good part of the magazine was written by Willa Cather. In addition, she began officially in the fall of 1893 to write drama reviews and weekly columns for the *Nebraska State Journal*, continuing in even more professional style after her graduation from the university in 1895. For several months she was an associate editor on a weekly paper, the Lincoln *Courier*, and throughout the year until June, 1896, a columnist and critic for either (sometimes both) the *Courier* and the *Journal*. Her long columns of comment on the arts—drama, music, books—often covered half a newspaper page. They were studded with names, allusions, telling observations—all in a restless, eager, knowing style. Willa Cather was a brilliant, forceful, intense, and richly gifted girl who—everybody knew—would of course do something in the world.

Although she worked miscellaneously at writing for the year after her graduation, and at least one story, "On the Divide," was published in a national magazine, the *Overland Monthly* (Jan., 1896),[5] for a while it must have seemed to Willa Cather that nothing *was* going to happen. Then she left in June, 1896, for Pittsburgh to be managing editor of the *Home Monthly*, a magazine which she proceeded to fill with or without contributors, under various pseudonyms, and in different styles. She also began in 1896 as a drama critic for the Pittsburgh *Leader*, going to that newspaper for a full-time position in the fall of 1897. From December, 1896, to the spring of 1900 she continued, with few interruptions, to send back her weekly column, "The Passing Show," first to the *Journal* and later to the *Courier*. During this period to 1900, Willa Cather used poems journalistically, or as incidental to her prose. There were lines quoted or composed, experiments in translation, and verse written for the *Home Monthly* as in her college days she had written jingles for the *Hesperian* or composed stories and verse for the younger children in her family.

Translations had begun during her Lincoln period, first the lines from Greek or Latin and then poems from modern Continental writers. One quotation from Alfred de Musset's *Rolla* (in an essay on Ruskin) may be her own.[6] And during the early Pittsburgh years she was involved in

5. Texts of all of Willa Cather's short stories mentioned throughout this introduction will be found in *Willa Cather's Collected Short Fiction, 1892–1912* [edited by Virginia Faulkner], with an introduction by Mildred R. Bennett (Lincoln: University of Nebraska Press, 1965), *passim*. This volume will be cited hereafter as *CSF*.

6. Eleven lines, beginning "Your world is superb, your men are perfect," and ending "But virtue is also dead, and we no longer believe in God" (*Nebraska State Journal*, hereafter cited as *Journal*, May 17, 1896; *KA*, p. 404).

simultaneously reading and translating with her friends Helen and George Seibel. One of their books, recalls George Seibel, was Musset's *Poésies Nouvelles*, "in which we read 'Rolla,' the various 'Nuits' of various months, the 'Letter to Malibran,' and other bits of melodious melancholia." They read Gautier, Flaubert, Verlaine, and Baudelaire, and "scaled towers of alexandrines in Victor Hugo's *Hernani*." Both Seibel and Dorothy Canfield Fisher have recalled Willa's translation of "The Three Holy Kings" from Heine, and though there are discrepancies in the time sequence as the events were remembered later, the poem must be the one on the illustrated front page of the *Home Monthly* for December, 1896. Mrs. Fisher wrote in 1947 to George Seibel: "Do you remember how delighted Willa and I were with the poem as you either read it or told it to us that evening? And afterwards Willa made a translation of it in rhyme— you remember she was a very good versifier at that time—and it was published in some magazine with a full-page illustration."[7] Other translations from Heine and Alfred de Musset appear in her newspaper columns.

One recurring device in the early articles (as well as in a few of Willa Cather's stories) is the use of a quotation or poem as an epigraph to a prose piece.[8] Sometimes the motif is only a line or two, sometimes a whole poem, but always it embodies a theme relevant to the larger work. Wilde's "Hélas!" and Poe's lines from his poem "For Annie" ("My tantalized spirit") precede her 1895 articles on those writers. In 1897, her first printed translation from Heine, "The Errand" ("Arise, arise, my trusty page"), introduces comment on a dispute about erecting a statue of Heine in Brooklyn. A stanza from Kipling's "Feet of the Young Men" introduces a piece on Fridtjof Nansen, the Arctic explorer. With the

7. George Seibel, "Miss Willa Cather from Nebraska," *New Colophon*, II (Sept., 1949), pp. 196-197 ff. Dorothy Canfield Fisher is quoted in Mildred R. Bennett, "Willa Cather in Pittsburgh," *Prairie Schooner*, XXXIII (Spring, 1959), 67. Mrs. George Seibel has told me that she can determine from other events recalled in their family that Dorothy Canfield's Christmas visit was definitely in 1897.

8. Quotations referred to in this paragraph are from Willa Cather's column, "The Passing Show," in the *Courier*, unless otherwise noted. (Some selections from these and other journalistic writings have been reprinted in *KA*; others will appear in the forthcoming collection, *The World and the Parish*, edited by William Curtin, to be published by the University of Nebraska Press.) References: Wilde (Sept. 28, 1895; *KA*, p. 390); Poe (Oct. 12, 1895; *KA*, pp. 380-381); Heine, "The Errand" (Nov. 6, 1897); Kipling (Dec. 18, 1897); Stevenson (Jan. 22, 1898; Oct. 21, 1899); Housman (Nov. 20, 1897; Feb.19, 1898; Apr. 23, 1898); Markham (Sept. 16, 1899); Heine (Jan. 6, 1900); on Tarkington (Jan. 20, 1900); Rossetti (*Journal*, Jan. 13, 1895; *KA*, p. 347). See also *KA*, pp. 93-99, 442-444, and *passim*. for additional discussion of Willa Cather's epigraphs to *The Troll Garden*.

account of Daudet's funeral in 1898, she quotes lines from Stevenson that also suggest her own poem "L'Envoi":

> I have trod the upward and the downward slope;
> And I have endured and done in days before;
> I have longed for all and bid farewell to hope;
> And I have lived and loved and shut the door.

This quotation, apparently a favorite, appears again with a discussion of Stevenson the following year. Housman is used several times: with a story on the McKinley parade in Pittsburgh ("The street sounds to the soldier's tread"), and an account of an actress and her daughter ("When, ah when, shall I be hid"); two stanzas of "To an Athlete Dying Young" are combined with a description of the funeral of Lt. F. W. Jenkins, whose body was brought home to Pittsburgh from Havana. Lines from Markham's "The Man with the Hoe" introduce a piece on Zola; lines from Heine ("In that voice what darker magic / Lurks to wake forgotten pain") lead into an article on the singer Clara Butt; some doggerel ("you can't make a man of a college star") precedes her review of Booth Tarkington's *A Gentleman from Indiana*. Willa Cather continued to use the device in later works: lines from Christina Rossetti's "Goblin Market" (called her "one perfect poem" in an 1895 article) as one of the epigraphs to her first book of prose, the stories of *The Troll Garden* (1905); a line from *Pan Tadeusz* by Adam Mickiewicz, as well as her own "Prairie Spring," for *O Pioneers!* (1913), and the title of the book itself as allusion to Whitman's poem.

In the context of motifs and epigraphs comes the first signed poem by Willa Cather to appear outside the early campus publications. Although verses accompany several of the early stories and articles, and can be attributed to the work as a whole, they are not separately signed. But in the *Courier* of April 22, 1899, a poem on the reality of illusion precedes an article on Richard Mansfield in the play *Cyrano de Bergerac*, and is signed "W. C." The poem begins, "Then back to ancient France again," and ends,

> Lift high the cup of Old Romance,
> And let us drain it to the lees;
> Forgotten be the lies of life,
> For these are its realities!

As one character had said in her 1896 story, "The Count of Crow's Nest," "'... the domain of pure art is always the indefinite. You want the fact under the illusion, whereas the illusion is in itself the most wonderful of facts.'"9

More interesting than the poems she wrote before 1900 are the ideas and judgments of poetry we find in Willa Cather's journalistic pieces. The serious comments do not begin auspiciously for a woman writer: In 1895 (Jan. 13) her column in the *Journal* told of the death of Christina Rossetti—a good poet but not the equal of her Pre-Raphaelite brother, Dante Gabriel, with his "enchanting style." In fact, writes Willa Cather, "It is a very grave question whether women have any place in poetry at all." To be any good, they must stay with subjective, emotional subjects. Christina Rossetti did know her limits and confined herself to "the simplest lyrics." Elizabeth Barrett Browning, on the other hand, was more intellectual; she "attempted all sorts of poetry and achieved merit without greatness." Sappho was the only great woman poet—particularly in "that one wonderful hymn to Aphrodite."10

During the following year and a half, while she was still in Nebraska, Willa Cather wrote often of poets and poetry.11 There were substantial articles on Wilde, Verlaine, Byron, Burns, Poe, Whitman—though often the emphasis was on the paradoxes of the poets' lives rather than on their poetry. Among other poets referred to and quoted were Swinburne, Shelley, Keats, Thomas Moore, Alfred de Musset, Gautier, Chatterton, Kipling, Heine, Stevenson, Browning, Tennyson, Shakespeare, and new writers like Richard Hovey and Bliss Carman. Her quotations range from the most familiar Shakespearean lines to passages from James Thomson's *The City of Dreadful Night*, or a sonnet by Philip Burke Marston.

A sampling of Willa Cather's comments during this early period may indicate the direction of her interests. Bad poets were those like Ella Wheeler Wilcox, "who wrote those scarlet sins called *Poems of Passion* and *Poems of Pleasure* in which she sings of 'dear, dead love' and makes 'pray' rhyme with 'America'"—or England's new Poet Laureate, Alfred Austin, who was "not a poet at all." Among good poets,

9. *CSF*, p. 453. "The Count of Crow's Nest" was first published in the *Home Monthly*, Sept.-Oct., 1896. For the text of the poem, "Then back to ancient France again," see Appendix.

10. *Journal*, Jan. 13, 1895; *KA*, pp. 346-349, 374-375.

11. Quotations mentioned in this and the following two paragraphs are from "The Passing Show." In the *Courier*: Thomson (Sept. 7, 1895; *KA*, p. 163); Marston (Sept. 14, 1895); Wilcox (Sept. 7, 1895). In the *Journal*: Austin and Swinburne (Jan. 19, 1896; *KA*, p. 192); Verlaine (Feb. 2, 1896; *KA*, pp. 394-396); Byron and Moore (Mar. 8, 1896; *KA*, p. 398); Hovey (Mar. 1, 1896; *KA*, p. 355); Whitman (Jan. 19, 1896; *KA*, pp. 351-353); Burns (May 24, 1896; *KA*, p. 344).

Swinburne has "achieved the impossible in English meters." Verlaine was "one of the greatest poets of modern France," she wrote at the time of his death in 1896, noting especially "the beauty of his rhythm and the incomparable grace and movement of his verse." He was "a colorist in phrases," his poems like jewels or light, "cold, beautiful and strangely inhuman." His verses are like music, made of harmony and feeling, "as indefinite and barren of facts as a nocturne"; words communicate not only by their meaning but by their "relation, harmony and sound." Willa Cather usually leaned to the poet as singer, and to a "Greek" ideal of art that was high and pure, but also intuitive and natural. Byron and Moore, for example, were "singers, rather than poets," and they were like the bards of Greece. Richard Hovey's new *Taliesin: A Masque* appealed greatly: it is "strong and clear and Greek," breathing "a higher and purer spirit of poetry than anything that has appeared since Browning's last poems and Swinburne's 'Atalanta in Calydon.'" Hovey, she thought, had the "pure lyric quality. . . . the poetry absolute and the sort of high noon meridian ecstasy that Keats and Shelley knew how to breathe into into song."

At the opposite of Verlaine's strict formulations of language and yet confusingly like the natural singers was Whitman. Her dialogue about him in January, 1896, may indicate a life-long argument in herself that would be reflected in the striking variations of both her prose and her poetry during the next twenty years. Whitman, she said, had the unreasoning enthusiasm of a boy, "a primitive elemental force . . . . hardiness and . . . joy of life." (Was this the primitive force of youth suggested later in the figures from their own past which haunted Bartley Alexander in *Alexander's Bridge* and Godfrey St. Peter in *The Professor's House*?) Still, Whitman had no discrimination, and, she thought, "the poet's task is usually to select the poetic." Whitman "looks at all nature in the delighted, admiring way in which the old Greeks and the primitive poets did"; he is sensual, barbaric, physical. And yet she did not feel that he always wrote poetry: "keen senses do not make a poet"; there must be the spiritual quality, there must be selection and form. In a slightly different way, a comment on Burns also foreshadows a choice: in a time "when English verse was most stiff and stilted, when literature consisted of the sparkling artificiality of the wits of Queen Anne's day," there awakened "out in the fields of Ayrshire that glorious voice . . . . Just a plow-boy, singing because the sun shone and maids were fair, and yet, with those spontaneous metres which the larks taught him, he gave new life to English verse." In tone, this is very much like the first critical reaction to O Pioneers! and its fresh, new world—O Pioneers! in which Whitman's presence is, at last, unmistakable.

The columns sent back from Pittsburgh after 1896 continue to reflect Willa Cather's reading and her ideas on writing.[12] One mentions a horse show, with horsewomen "from all over These States as Walt Whitman put it." Among other writers mentioned are Stevenson, Housman, Rossetti, Lewis Carroll, Musset, Byron, Browning, Kipling, Markham, Rostand. She liked a volume of poetry by Yone Noguchi. There are several articles on Richard Realf, Pittsburgh poet and adventurer, in which she takes the same point of view as in her earlier pieces on Wilde and Verlaine, defending the poetry in spite of the poet's life. And she continued to make distinctions: Kipling is a good, enjoyable poet, she wrote, but compare even his best verse with the first book of Hyperion or the best parts of Sordello, and he becomes mere opera bouffe, vaudeville. "There is something tremendously virile and effective about those loose, vivid phrases of his, and one need not be ashamed to feel their spell, but for all that they are not the language of the hill of Helicon." She liked Bliss Carman's The Aurelian Wall and Other Poems, a book of elegies ("not so much of the great dead as the dear dead"), and she quoted his poems on Stevenson and Verlaine. She did not like Stephen Crane's War Is Kind, although it is implied that The Black Riders was much better—"a casket of polished masterpieces" in comparison. W. B. Yeats's The Wind Among the Reeds introduced another problem. Except as duty, she says, "I would never read, or even begin to read, a volume of poetry with 43 pages of notes, nor do I care to study Celtic myths in verse. Poetry that has to be explained, by its author's own confession, usually would be as well unwritten." Yet Yeats can write real poetry, and she quotes "The Cap and Bells" as "the best of the book, because it relates an experience of the heart, illumines a little the comedy of life, and can be read without notes by the simplest . . . ."

12. Articles mentioned in this and the following four paragraphs are either from "The Passing Show" in the Courier or the Journal, all signed "Willa Cather," or from reviews in the Pittsburgh Leader, signed "Sibert" or identified by other publication and reference: Horse show (Courier, Oct. 23, 1897); Yone Noguchi (Leader, Dec. 31, 1897, unsigned; reprinted Courier, Jan. 29, 1898); Richard Realf ("Genius in Mire," Leader, Feb. 12, 1899, p. 20, reprinted with slight additions, Courier, Feb. 25, 1899; also Courier, Apr. 8, 1899, in which Willa Cather identifies as hers the unsigned piece, "Mrs. Realf's Story," Leader, Feb. 15, 1899, p. 6 ["That's what it cost me to marry a poet," concluded Mrs. Realf.]); Kipling (Journal, May 16, 1897); Carman (Leader, July 22, 1898); Crane and Yeats (Leader, June 3, 1899); Lohengrin (Courier, June 10, 1899); Nevin (Courier, July 15, 1899); Housman (Courier, Mar. 10, 1900); poets (Journal, May 16, 1897); Phillips (Courier, Mar. 3, 1900).

Two comments in 1899 illustrate Willa Cather's reluctance to intellectualize and factualize poetry and art. In a piece on *Lohengrin*, she says that joy is not to be analyzed. In one scene of the opera, Elsa asks for "the name"—"Well, she got it, and so do the people who construct systems for measuring the value of poetry, but at what cost! They get the name, and perhaps acquire vast erudition, but they lose the knight, and Mount Monsalvat, and the bright temple of the Grail and all the rest of it." The thing that is not there and which comes from beyond the page or the object is what she called sometimes the "aroma" of language or sound or line, as in her comment on Ethelbert Nevin's music: It has an "aroma of poetry, a breath from some world brighter and better than ours."

In one essay, "A Lyric Poet," she compares the scholarly but unpoetic verse of George E. Woodberry with the natural and authentic lyricism of a poet then new to her—A. E. Housman:

> There is nothing so unmistakable as a true poem; there is nothing over which the conventions of men and the laws of the schools have so little control as poetry. . . . A man can no more write a poem by mastering poetics than a botanist can make a rose, or an astronomer fashion a star. . . . The true poem is and must remain largely a happy accident. . . .

The gift of the true poet is "a certain touch of divinity in man. . . . a man either is a poet or he is not." *A Shropshire Lad* had been published only recently, in 1896, but Willa Cather had already found it a book to love: "I do not know who Mr. Housman is, but I know that he is a poet." She had not been able to find out anything about him. But the lads and lassies of Shropshire are real, though they came to such sad endings. "One lad, an athlete, died young, before the laurel of his triumphs had withered, and his sweetheart married his best friend." Housman must have wandered to London, she thought, an exile in the city ("Here I lie down in London / And turn to rest alone"). Housman's is true poetry—"there is a touch as genuine as Heine's, an expression simple, complete, perfect." Every lyric has "absolute genuineness. This Shropshire lad has an existence in literature as actual and indisputable as Childe Harold's. This homesick boy is one of the dwellers on Helicon." She quotes "On your midnight pallet lying, / Listen, and undo the door! . . ." and says, "That is what it means to write poetry: to be able to say the oldest thing in the world as though it had never been said before." She quotes also the light poem, "When I was one and twenty," but returns to the homesick songs she likes the best: "'Tis time, I think, by Wenlock town / The golden broom should blow...." Perhaps some of her own homesickness creeps in as she describes the exile in the city who has "wept for the west wind and the brown fields and the quiet country stars. And in so far, many of us are his brothers in exile."

The divinity of poetry and the immanence of the gods had long been assumed. "In all ages and in all tongues," she had written several years earlier, "whether they wrote epics or lyrics, Bibles or love songs, poets have struggled with something beyond the human, with the unreasonable and inexplicable unrest which gives us our highest and most unreasonable hope." But at the turn of the century, poetry seemed to be a little short of greatness. Stephen Phillips' dramatic poem *Paola and Francesca*, she says, is not a great play, though the poetry has great beauty—the poet "is a true son of Apollo and of the Royal House of Song." His melody is perhaps equal to Tennyson's, and it has an even "wilder, sweeter and sadder music" that is like Keats but without his "warm, sensuous joyousness." After reading Phillips, she says, "I took down my Keats and read *Lamia* over again and thought the hand had not yet been made that could erase that great name writ in water."

In 1900, Willa Cather began some serious publishing in both fiction and poetry. Eleven signed poems appeared in 1900, two in 1901, four in 1902, and *April Twilights* in 1903. Of course many of the poems of 1900 were drawn to print by the demands of a new (and short-lived) literary magazine in Pittsburgh, the *Library*, to which Willa Cather and George Seibel were the chief contributors. The first of her later collected poems to be printed was "Thou Art the Pearl," published in the *Library* (March 24, 1900) under one of her various pseudonyms, "John Charles Asten." The first to be recognized in a magazine outside Cather's editorial interests was the popular "'Grandmither, Think Not I Forget,'" in the *Critic* (April, 1900), and many times reprinted. Two others of some home or western interest were the lively "Broncho Bill's Valedictory" and the lines about her brother Jack, "Are You Sleeping, Little Brother?" A poem called "Aftermath" also appeared in the *Library*, but, except for the last five lines, it was completely revised before it was used in *April Twilights*.

Willa Cather was enjoying considerable success. The poems were printed in national magazines (*Lippincott's*, *Harper's Weekly*, *Youth's Companion*, *Critic*, *Current Literature*), and some of them were reprinted at home in the *Courier* ("In the Night," "'Grandmither, Think Not I Forget,'" "Broncho Bill's Valedictory," "Are You Sleeping, Little Brother?"). Friends in Nebraska were impressed and delighted. Two reprints of 1902 in the *Courier* brought admiring comment from the editor, Sarah B. Harris: Of "Arcadian Winter" (Jan. 18) she wrote: "The exquisite rhythm and the tender memoriam for skies that look bluer now than when they domed Arcady is characteristic. The grace and music and regret of the lines haunt one like the idyls of Herrick." "The Namesake" (Apr. 12) was praised for "the vividness and the realization of youth and the passion of patriotism and of kindred." And yet, even with publication and growing praise, some of Willa Cather's poems in this period have a mood of unrest and uncertainty. For example, "Winter in Delphi," with Apollo absent from the House of Song, may reflect her own justified questions: After all the expectations, what was she really to become? A cluster of short stories, reams of journalism, some poems—but where was the great thing, the true light of Apollo? As she was to write of Thea Kronborg some years later in *The Song of the Lark*, "she had an appointment to meet the rest of herself sometime, somewhere."

In the spring of 1901, Willa Cather had begun to teach in the Pittsburgh high schools. She was living at the home of her friend Isabelle McClung, where she had a separate room in the attic for work, and the writing developed more strongly. Poems came out of significant events in this period. The death of Ethelbert Nevin on February 17, 1901, gave the elegy "Sleep, Minstrel, Sleep" and the related "Arcadian Winter" and "Song." Others came out of events in Red Cloud that summer ("The Night Express") and from experiences on a trip to Europe with Isabelle McClung in the summer of 1902. Finally a collection of poems, published and unpublished, was prepared. At about the same time, Willa Cather indicated in one newspaper article that she agreed with those critics who thought that the trend of American poetry was toward the brief, restrained, and carefully wrought lyric.[13]

April Twilights was published in late April, 1903, by Richard G. Badger through the Gorham Press (and distributed in Pittsburgh by J. R. Weldin): "52 pages. Price, cloth, $1.00." The *Nebraska State Journal* for May 18, 1903 announced "a collection of poems by Willa Sibert Cather, formerly dramatic critic on this paper and later of the staff of the Lincoln Courier and of the Pittsburgh Leader." The poems "possess a quiet charm very appropriately suggested in the title. The Journal hails her first

13. "Poets of Our Younger Generation," Pittsburgh *Gazette* (Nov. 30, 1902), reports and comments on an earlier article by Josephine Dodge Daskam, "The Distinction of Our Poetry," *Atlantic Monthly*, LXXXVII (May, 1901), 696–705, and by the title refers to William Archer's *Poets of the Younger Generation* (London: John Lane, 1902), then being widely reviewed.

book with delight and feels sure that it is but the harbinger of many future achievements of her facile pen." A sketch of the author's life "on a ranch in southwestern Nebraska and later in Red Cloud where she ran wild some years before beginning her school education" had been sent by the publisher.

Perhaps the first review was that by George Seibel on his book page of the Pittsburgh *Gazette*, appearing with a picture of Willa Cather on April 26, 1903. *April Twilights* was called "a book of genuine poetry in unpretentious guise, unheralded by sounding bugles, but singing its way straight to the heart of every one who looks within its covers." He notes an echo of Sappho, a perfection of form that reminds one of Gautier. A few errors are noted, but in general the verse is "immaculate and musical," direct, simple, and sensuous. Miss Cather "disdains luxuriant words, and with homely Anglo-Saxon syllables paints pictures that will not fade." She has restraint and temperance, is not one of the "dictionary topers." Even when she "treads upon Swinburne's holy ground she wisely refrains from his fanfarons and flourishes." Poems printed in full are "Aftermath" and "On Cydnus"; "The Tavern" and "Winter in Delphi" are especially admired (the latter, he says, has much in common with Swinburne's "Last Oracle"). "London Roses," however, is not poetry. The book shows her feeling for nature—"everywhere vital and near—it is not a painted and perfumed nature"; the poems have a "haunting melancholy.... Like the lament for the vanished god, unresponding, unreturning, there is an undertone of pensive sadness." He concludes that *April Twilights* is "a volume that will firmly fix her literary reputation, now confined to the ephemeral pages of magazines where even a prolific author is lost in the crowd."

Another strong review of *April Twilights* appeared in the *New York Times Saturday Review* for June 20, 1903. It was discussed in "Recent Poetry," an unsigned article on three of the books that had come from Richard G. Badger that spring. "Her gift is genuine," said the reviewer of Willa Cather, "her performance already beautiful, and giving promise of an unfolding to be looked for with eagerness." He speaks of Miss Cather's "variety of metres" and "delicate, whimsical charm." Although he likes "In Media Vita" best, for its "unaffected simplicity," he quotes "Winter in Delphi" because it is more representative—it "gives perhaps as well as anything its author's native note." He thinks that she is perhaps "overfond of lilting measures for a poet with so much insight to the sadder side of human experience," but "it is impossible to read her more successful pieces without recognizing the firm and delicate conception underlying the musical and suggestive phrasing." In a specific comment, he suggests that the word "defile" in "The Tavern" should be replaced with "despoil"; and he quotes the entire poem "to show the quality of her metaphor in presenting a familiar feeling."

The reviews in other magazines and papers[14] were mostly passive. Some praised the book, often for irrelevant reasons; some found it undistinguished. Reading them now, one is struck by the often inappropriate and even false judgments in the reviews, their authors betrayed into wordage by the column inch. (This was a hazard Willa Cather knew only too well.) She must have hated some of the comments: "That *musis amicus,*—the befriender of the yet uncommissioned troubadour—the muse yet uncrowned,—we refer to Mr. Richard Badger,—has rendered no truer service than in introducing this shy, wistful, and winsome singer who here puts forth her maiden effort" (*Critic*). It was true, of course, that the Badger books were made from solicited and often self-subsidized manuscripts of young writers; they poured in streams over the desks of the reviewers, and were often mentioned only in roundup reviews. That *April Twilights* had a number of special mentions is to its credit.

From the reviewers: "Once in a while one happens upon a work of a real poet," wrote Jeannette L. Gilder in the Chicago *Tribune*. She quoted "'Grandmither, Think Not I Forget'" (which—though she did not mention the fact—had first been published in the magazine edited by Miss Gilder, the *Critic*). The comments by the Boston *Evening Transcript* have special interest because the "two bits of genuine sentiment" that are selected for praise are poems Cather later rejected. "'The Night Express,'" said the reviewer, "is a picture of the iron horse which stirs the restless hearts of village boys, and taking them out into the great world at last, in death, brings them home again. The other poem 'The Namesake' invests our Civil War period with reality, as it depicts the soldier who lies on a Southern battlefield." The *Dial* found the title of "no particular sig-

14. I have read the following reviews: George Seibel, "A Pittsburgh Poet's Volume of Verse," Pittsburgh *Gazette* (April 26, 1903), sec. 2, p. 4; *Nebraska State Journal* (May 11, 1903), 6; Jeannette L. Gilder, Chicago *Tribune* (May 23, 1903), 9; New York *Times Saturday Review* (June 20, 1903), 434; *Bookman*, XVII (July, 1903), 542; Edith M. Thomas, "Recent Books of Poetry," *Critic*, XLIII (July, 1903), 81; *Dial*, XXXV (July 16, 1903), 40–41; *Academy and Literature*, LXV (July 18, 1903), 57; Boston *Evening Transcript* (Aug. 12, 1903), 16; *Poet Lore*, XIV (Winter, 1903), 113-115; *Book News*, XXII (Dec., 1903), 541; *Criterion*, IV (Oct., 1903), 53; Rafford Pyke, *Bookman*, XIX (Apr., 1904), 196; and a comment by Ferris Greenslet, *Under the Bridge* (Boston: Houghton Mifflin Company, 1943), p. 116.

nificance, unless it suggests the subdued tone of her tranquil musings."
"Prairie Dawn" is "pretty enough to quote." He concludes, "Of such
exquisite description there is much in Miss Cather's collection; there are
also engaging reflections from the world of books, the history, and the
legend of the ages." An English magazine (*Academy and Literature*) thought
the book better than most others of the group of minor poems from
Boston it was reviewing. It has "some tenderness, some music, and some
originality. Nowhere does the verse reach a high level, but it is seldom
bathetic and never silly. Miss Cather, too, can get a lilt into her lines
which has something of the real singing quality." This review quotes
"Mills of Montmartre," another poem excluded from the 1923 *April
Twilights*. The *Criterion* liked "The Tavern," which has "a quaint
beauty like some of the well-known minor poems of the seventeenth
century." A year later, the *Bookman* has, "Miss Willa Cather writes very
well indeed," and quotes "Prairie Dawn" to illustrate. But in some real
lint-picking, the reviewer objects to the word "conjure" in "Aftermath"
and questions the necessity of the note to "Mills of Montmartre." There
is a record of one other review. Ferris Greenslet in *Under the Bridge* (1943)
recalls his first meeting with Willa Cather and comments: "In free-lance
days, I had reviewed a thin volume of verse, of which one piece had
haunted my memory. It ended with a strain of New-Celtic mysticism,"
and he quotes from the last stanza of "I Sought the Wood in Winter."

One of the most spectacular reviews was a full-page article in *Poet
Lore*, in a section called "Present Day Glimpses of Poets," with a picture
of "Willa Sibert Cather" in a light dress with tie, seated sideways on a
bench (see frontispiece). The article is part biography, part criticism. It
was no doubt intended to publicize the book, since the Gorham Press,
which printed the Badger books, also published *Poet Lore*. Because Willa
Cather was certainly consulted about the article, it does have some
valuable information on the poems. It says that all of the verse was done
in the last five years, that Cather's "early effort was all toward prose."
Willa Cather thinks that "'Grandmither'" is the best poem. It was
"never retouched after the first writing" (but see Notes on the Poems).
In addition, Miss Cather selected "Mills of Montmartre" and "The
Hawthorn Tree" as favorites.

A number of the poems in *April Twilights* were subsequently published in other magazines, but the book itself had little circulation.
Finally, Willa Cather herself bought up and destroyed the remaining
copies ("all stray copies bought up and buried," she told Elizabeth

Shepley Sergeant), afterward growing increasingly cold to her early work.[15] By 1923 she was ready to reissue the book as *April Twilights and Other Poems*, including twelve poems published during those twenty years. When she cut out thirteen of the original poems, it is curious indeed that she would leave out "Mills of Montmartre" when she had selected it as one of her best. But her tastes and judgments were to change. In a statement in the *Poetry Review* (1925) she chose all her favorites from the new group. The author of the article, however, recalls the first *April Twilights*—"a slim book of poetry filled with her woods in winter, white birches, evening songs and laments, legends and taverns and hawthorne trees, the night express and rose time."[16] Yet this, too, after twenty years, did not give a clear view of the early book.

In spite of its apparent obscurity, the 1903 *April Twilights* may have played another significant role in Willa Cather's career. It is generally assumed that her relationship with *McClure's* began with Mr. McClure's interest in her manuscripts and his visit to see her in Pittsburgh in 1904 or 1905, to be followed by the publication of *The Troll Garden* (1905), and the subsequent steady movement to success through her work on the magazine and her later novels. But in the *Nebraska State Journal* of May 11, 1903, is a news item from New York that changes the date: "Miss Willa Cather of Pittsburgh . . . was in the city this week. She was summoned by the McClure people, who have of late taken a lively interest in her literary work. It is said that an arrangement has been made for the publication of some of her stories in the magazine." It would take more than a year for "The Sculptor's Funeral" and "Paul's Case" to appear in *McClure's*, but as early as 1903 something had happened. And, coincidentally, it happened a few weeks after the publication of her first book. Could it have been *April Twilights* after all that gave Willa Cather a new door to open?

2

In *April Twilights* one moves in a mythic landscape. Figures of gods and god-men perform the rituals of legend in pastoral Arcadia, the world of Roman glory, or scenes from medieval balladry and romance. But the Virgilian shepherds and minstrels blend into the equally indefinite "lads" of Housman, who had his own elegiac tone; Arcadia is also Shropshire

15. *Willa Cather: A Memoir* (Revised edition; Lincoln: University of Nebraska Press, 1963), p. 52.

16. See note 1, above, pp. 407-408.

and Provence, with life shown in allegory. The classical-pastoral scene is overlaid with a glitter of plumes and swords and roses from the mythical kingdom of Ruritania—a glow that might be called "Zenda-romantic." For there is in Willa Cather a good deal of her much-read, much-loved *Prisoner of Zenda*, with its far-away, heroic action and its bittersweet ending of unfulfilled love. The poems also have something of the neo-Greek or medieval tone of Rossetti, Swinburne, and Wilde, and more than a touch of Wagnerian story and song. Near by is the world of the early Yeats, minstrel poet of the Celtic twilight and "old earth's dreamy youth."

The subjects of the poems show Willa Cather's rich interests—literature, art, music, places of the world, memories of home—and her ready response to the particular emotional aura of the experience. Yet the poems seldom record an encounter with immediate fact: the real (or inner) action is usually elsewhere. Even the most direct poems lead to other times and places. London roses are "perfumed with a thousand years," Ludlow Castle means Sir Philip Sidney, the express train brings home the lads who wandered. The boys of "Dedicatory" lie dreaming in the past. This kind of focus does not lessen the subjects; it merely defines the nature of the poems. They are symbolic, made of the illusion that Cather in that early poem—"Then back to ancient France"—had called the greatest reality.

For poetic materials, Willa Cather went first to the tradition of pastoral primitivism, which assumed a golden age in the past: the idealized Arcadian land of gods, shepherds, and song. She entered with Virgil, as he says in the opening lines of the *Georgics*, Book III:

You too, great goddess of sheepfolds, I'm going to sing, and you
Apollo, a shepherd once, and the woods and streams of Arcadia.

With Virgil she could say, "I must venture a theme will exalt me / From earth and give me wings and a triumph on every tongue." Then follows the line in the *Georgics* that has so often been identified with Cather: "I'll be the first to bring the Muse of song to my birthplace."[17]

The Arcadian metaphors were familiar to poets from Theocritus and Virgil to the Elizabethans. In the Age of Reason, the pastoral figures became more deliberately quaint, formal, and dispassionate; but with Keats (his Grecian urn has men and gods of "Tempe and the dales of Arcady"), and finally with Yeats, they took on a shadowy melancholy

17. All quotations from the *Georgics* are from *The Georgics of Virgil*, translated by C. Day Lewis (New York: Oxford University Press, 1947).

for that lost, bright world. "The woods of Arcady are dead," Yeats wrote in "The Song of the Happy Shepherd" (1889). The term "Arcady" was not unusual in the fiction and poetry at the turn of the century. So Willa Cather also used the terms of the tradition in such poems as "Arcadian Winter," "Winter at Delphi," "Lament for Marsyas," and "I Sought the Wood in Winter." The last poem, however, is a pastoral study of cyclic time (summer and winter, flowers and snow) that ends on the hard snow peaks of the mountains that lifted from the Arcadian fields: "Behind the rose the planet, / The Law behind the veil." We find in the poems all the usual figures of Arcadia—Apollo and Pan; minstrels, shepherds, huntsmen, runners of races; laurels and daffodils. In addition the troubadour's lute and the trumpets of Zenda make variations in other poems ("The Encore," "I Have No House for Love to Shelter Him," "The Poor Minstrel," "Thou Art the Pearl"). "Poppies on Ludlow Castle" and "The Namesake" have a chivalric tone. All these invoke a golden age, gone with the minstrels who sang it.

Her deep involvement with the Arcadian theme and her identification of singer and poet are clearly demonstrated in what she wrote about Ethelbert Nevin.[18] She had met him early in her Pittsburgh years, had delighted in his company, his music, and his family, and had altogether idealized him as a modern troubadour of remarkable beauty and genius. She wrote in 1898 that the "shepherd boys who piped in the Vale of Tempe centuries agone might have looked like that, or Virgil's Menaclas, when he left his flock beneath the spreading beech tree and came joyous to the contest of song." Nevin died on February 17, 1901, a loss more poignant because of his youth (he was 39, but looked like a boy). In her article on his death, Willa Cather first quoted Housman: "Lie down, lie down, young yeoman." Whom the gods love die young—"indeed it was almost impossible to conceive of his outliving his youth, or that there should ever come a winter in his Arcady." She had heard his music at a concert the preceding April. Some of the same songs were sung at his funeral, "when the snow was driving outside and 'the land was white with winter.'" It was also the world's lost youth she lamented, and the modern poet's misalliance with society. Nevin "was as incongruous here as though he had strayed out of a Greek pastoral with a flower wreathed crook, so that he seemed to the eyes of the vulgar to be always in masquerade. Out of the soot-drift of the factories and amid the roar of the mills where the battle ships are forged, he sang his songs of youth and

18. *Courier*, Feb. 5, 1898; *Journal*, Mar. 24, 1901.

Arcady and summertime." These contrasts of summer and winter, the artist and the world, she recapitulates in "Arcadian Winter" and "Sleep, Minstrel, Sleep."

In other modifications of the Arcadian theme, Willa Cather followed Housman's treatment of the "lightfoot lads" in the fields of Shropshire who loved and warred, and often died while yet in summer glory. (What she did not know at the time was that Housman, himself a classical scholar, was using Arcadia in his own way.) Her "Lament for Marsyas" is most strongly Housman, repeating his "To an Athlete Dying Young." But here she uses Greek myth as subject—the story of the young singer Marsyas (also a shepherd in Arcady) who dueled with Apollo and lost. This poem has also a specific personal source. While she was in Arles in 1902, she saw a Latin sculpture, a triplex bas-relief, in the wall of the old Roman theater. In the center is the poet, striking his lyre in triumph. At the left is Apollo, sharpening his knife on a stone. At the right is Marsyas (the poet), hanging by his flayed hands from an oak tree, defeated.[19]

Other myths appear in the poems. "Eurydice" dramatizes insubstantial, unrealized love, and the human failure of Orpheus to fulfill the enchantment. The poem must have recalled to her the shadowy figures of Hell, lost on the river Avernus, as Virgil retells the story of Orpheus and Eurydice at the close of the *Georgics*. Both Eurydice and, in "Asphodel," the "pale shade in glorious battle slain," dreaming on the fields of Hades, are exiles from Arcadia. The invocation to Apollo in "Winter at Delphi" is to an absent god. These themes of separation and frustration turn everything a little to the dark half of the moon—the woman who cannot love, the man who cannot live, the artist who may not create.

The same theme of flawed inspiration comes in the Shakespearean metaphor of "Paradox"—it was Caliban, not Ariel, who sang. But the Shakespearean drama which most appealed to Willa Cather was that of Antony and Cleopatra. "On Cydnus" telescopes their history, as she found it in Plutarch, Shakespeare, and Lemprière's *Classical Dictionary*. It will be remembered that in Shakespeare's play, after being commanded to appear before Antony in Cilicia, Cleopatra "pursed up his heart upon

19. *Journal*, Oct. 19, 1902. Willa Cather's articles on her travels in Europe in 1902 were first published in the *Journal*, later reprinted in *Willa Cather in Europe*, with introduction and notes by George N. Kates (New York: Alfred A. Knopf, 1956). Dates and text used here and in the following discussion are from the *Journal*.

the river of Cydnus." When she came sailing up that river, "the barge she sat in, like a burnished throne, / Burned on the water" (*Antony and Cleopatra*, II, ii). In later times, it is the departure of her ships from the great naval battle between Antony and Caesar near Actium that scuttles their kingdoms:

> The noble ruin of her magic, Antony,
> Claps on his sea-wing, and like a doting mallard,
> Leaving the fight in height, flies after her.
>
> (III, x)

Lemprière tells of the legend that at a banquet in Alexandria, Cleopatra melted pearls in the wine to add richness to the occasion. Cather unifies these elements in the story with a vivid metaphor: The pearl dropped into the wine foreshadows the world that Antony would cast "into the wine-dark sea."

By far the largest part of her material came from literature, not only Shakespeare and the classics but also the songs of Villon and Béranger, Keats's *Endymion* and *Hyperion*, and modern works like Daudet's *Kings in Exile*, Heine's *The Gods in Exile*, or portions of *The North Sea*, in which Heine describes the lost gods. Sometimes the themes of myth and story focus on a statue or a painting. One such poem is "Antinous," a haunting piece with considerable complexity. For the speaker studies a statue that seems to breathe its own legend—like Keats's figures from the urn, or like Browning's painting of the "last Duchess" ("There she stands / As if alive"). The story is of the Emperor Hadrian's favorite, Antinous, his mysterious death (Was he drowned in the Nile?), and his subsequent deification. The description seems to be of the statue of Antinous in the Farnese collection in Naples. Though she did not visit Naples until 1908, Cather must have seen pictures or replicas of this statue, for there in marble as in the poem are the head bent slightly, the brooding eyes, the downcast posture—even the stick held in one hand, as was customary in representations of gods like Osiris.

A painter who appealed strongly to her was the English artist, Sir Edward Coley Burne-Jones. One of her travel accounts of 1902 (Aug. 17) describes a visit to his studio in London, and her story "The Marriage of Phaedra" (1905) echoes the experience. She had known about him as early as 1895, reporting in her *Journal* column of January 20 that the scenery of the "Passing of Arthur" (then being performed at the Lyceum theatre, London) had been painted by Burne-Jones. The poem "White Birch in

Wyoming" (though it goes off into the Wagnerian world) begins with a western scene described as "Stark as a Burne-Jones vision of despair"— perhaps like a scene envisioned for the "Passing of Arthur." However, a landscape with specific aptness forms the background of Burne-Jones's picture, "Mirror of Venus." It is indeed like parts of Wyoming—three ridges of barren hills and valleys. At the right of the picture is a cluster of white-trunked, tall, slim trees like birches. In the foreground are ten Pre-Raphaelite girls looking into a pool of water. In Cather's poem the tree comes into the foreground and becomes Brunhilda in exile from her northern Valkyr sisters. The wasteland remains, but the pool is only echoed: heat has drained the living water dry. In a book of text and prints which Cather might have seen, Malcolm Bell's *Edward Burne-Jones* (1892), the artist's landscapes are called "dream-lands of the earth, yet not earthly."

The spring poem "Fides, Spes" recalls another Burne-Jones painting —actually two, the panels called "Spes" and "Fides." Fides (Faith) is a woman watching a lamp, though the serpent of doubt is coiled around a staff at the side. Spes (Hope) is a woman with a branch of apple blossoms, pictured against a barred window and distant towers of a walled town.

Other Burne-Jones pictures might have become a part of Willa Cather's imagination. He has a series called "The Seasons," in which autumn is painted with a rocky, gull-haunted shore. "Spring" pictures Apollo with his feet on the clouds; he is laurel-crowned and playing his lyre. (See "Winter in Delphi" for Apollo and spring.) Burne-Jones also used the subjects of two myths which entered into Cather's work: Pyramus and Thisbe, and Orpheus.[20]

Poems that drew especially on experiences during Willa Cather's summer in Europe can be annotated from the travel articles she wrote for the *Journal*.

Visiting Ludlow, she remarked that Housman was not the only singing Shropshire lad. Sir Philip Sidney was there before him, his home in that castle. "Poppies on Ludlow Castle" memorializes the scene and the old heroic singing days. In her article of July 27 she mentions blooming alder trees and dog roses, but not poppies. Ludlow was country and the past, but London was city and the present, as it is described in "London Roses." There was the "court-born, alley-nursed, street bred girl"

20. For additional comment on Willa Cather's use of myth and classical allusion in her prose, see *KA*, pp. 97-103. An article by L. V. Jacks, "The Classics and Willa Cather," appeared in *Prairie Schooner*, XXXV (Winter, 1961-1962), pp. 289-296.

selling "Rowses, Rowses," her voice "harder than her gin-sodden face." But the depressing "London shoddy" were everywhere: "the streets are a restless, breathing, mal-odorous pageant of the seedy of all nations" (Aug. 10).

Three poems come from France. "Paris" praises "the city of delight," arrayed by her kings "with pride and power." As she wrote of the city in her article of Sept. 14, "Nearly every street in Paris bears the name of a victory—either of arms or intellect." "Mills of Montmartre" describes the "other days," before the Latin Quarter moved in. In Provence, the pastoral folk ways were still alive, with shepherds singing the old stories. In that golden countryside, and in the former Roman city of Arles, the "Provençal Legend" might have been told (Oct. 19).

The scene of "From the Valley" suggests the pine-covered, snow-topped Alps beyond Avignon—though the same ideas were also associated with American mountains and valleys. At Avignon, she wrote, the popes could "watch the Alps with one eye, and with the other look down upon the Rhone, the great highway to Italy, where every day barges and galleys went leaping down the current to Naples" (Sept. 28). The poem has a similar duality: on the heights, the gods are in their "imperishable seats," while in the valley "our days go by / Like shining water, coming not again." The poem is also a reminder of the Arcadia of Virgil's *Eclogue* X, where gods lived in the mountains, the "Pine-mantled Maenalus and stony steeps / Of cold Lycaeus."

Not many of the poems of *April Twilights* come from the American West. The setting of "White Birch in Wyoming" is technically in Wyoming, but the real relationship is to Burne-Jones and Wagner. "Prairie Dawn," however, catches in eight exact lines of remarkable swiftness the look and feel of the open prairie. The sage and the huddled herd suggest a landscape farther west than Red Cloud—more like Colorado or Wyoming, a country Willa Cather had visited during this early period. And the nostalgia of the concluding line, "A sudden sickness for the hills of home," is probably for something farther east than Nebraska. There are bluffs along the river at Red Cloud and rough terrain in parts of Webster County, but the shock of separation that first affected Willa Cather deeply was in her childhood experience of going from the wooded hills and mountains of Virginia to the hard, flat country of the Nebraska Divide ("I would not know how much a child's life is bound up in the woods and hills and meadows around it, if I had not been jerked away from all these and thrown out into a country as bare as a piece of sheet iron.")[21] It is also like the tone of her former teacher, Herbert Bates, whose *Songs of Exile* looked always toward the east, as he wrote in "Prairie"—"Back to the pine-clad hills of home." In fact, the phrase "hills of home" runs like a litany through several of the Bates poems. Song, he wrote, "homes" on hills. Bates could describe the Nebraska country vividly, as Cather was to do in later years; but in his view it was hard and raw, scorched with winds and the glare of sunflowers. In her poems Willa Cather was not ready to place Nebraska in the foreground, or to let it be in her imagination the "wild land" she loved.

Four poems (three of which she later rejected) come from her family and home life. "'Grandmither, Think Not I Forget'" is a love poem, invoking at the same time the memory of her grandmother Rachel E. Boak, who lived with the Cathers in Red Cloud and helped take care of the children. "Grandma" Boak had died in June, 1893. "The Namesake" comes also from the feeling of family and the roots of the blood, an identification of the young "Willie" Cather with her uncle William Sibert Boak who died at nineteen in the Civil War. "The Night Express" is based on the death of young Amos Cowden in the summer of 1901, when Willa Cather was home in Red Cloud. One night the body of the former Red Cloud boy was brought back to the familiar railroad station, his friends waiting on the platform as the train "Shoots red from out the marshes to bring a rover home." Perhaps most intimately connected with Willa Cather's early life and her later achievement are the dedicatory lines of *April Twilights*, addressed to her brothers Roscoe Clark Cather and Charles Douglass Cather—the "three who lay and planned at moonrise, / On an island in a western river." That sand bar in the river near Red Cloud was the early center of Willa Cather's creative imagination and the symbol of first dreams. But the tone of the poem is elegiac. The young men of "The Namesake" and "The Night Express" were dead; so the children of "Dedicatory" have faded into a vanished kingdom. What Orpheus now could summon them out of the shadows?

There is another group of somewhat ambivalent poems, notably the graceful "The Hawthorn Tree," "Aftermath," and "Thine Advocate." These lyrics may be personal, but they have an almost deliberate vagueness. In these love poems, unlike those of Rossetti, for example, one does not sense another person near or see the definite outline of any features.

21. *KA*, p. 448, reprinting an interview from the Philadelphia *Record*, dated Aug. 9, 1913.

There is the same separation and loss that the Arcadian poems and the home poems made thematic. "L'Envoi," on the contrary, has the sound of truth: "Where are the loves that we have loved before / When once we are alone and shut the door?" The self, the door, and the inner room are real—not in the elegiac and haunting April twilight but in a final darkness.

And what, in general, did Willa Cather choose for a poetic style? To our ear, the poems have a slightly old-fashioned tone. Even in 1903 they would have seemed familiar, for, at least in her early poetry, she was not an innovator. She took the given ways, with both grace and passion. Once she said in an early column that poetry "is retrospective; life precedes it always. Homer could only have written after the heroic age, not before it . . . . Our poets are always a generation or two behind us."[22] If this is true in part for the poet, it is, of course, not always apparent to his public. Often the great poet is a generation or two ahead of his time; the listening ear takes that long to be tuned. What she meant, no doubt, was that she found her creative impulse in her relationship with the past. And so, at this time, she wrote formal, Victorian-Georgian lyrics in conventional patterns, strongly marked with Pre-Raphaelite images and music (though hers were mauve and rose compared to the full-blooded purple of Swinburne, Rossetti, and FitzGerald). George Seibel recalls the time Willa brought some of her manuscripts to read—some of the poems later collected in *April Twilights*: "I can still remember the velvet cadence of her voice as she read 'Winter at Delphi' and 'Aftermath,' two sugared sonnets which neither of us then realized were begotten by Swinburne and Rossetti. Other poems had a drop of absinthe from Verlaine, whom we had been reading, or wine-wet rose petals from FitzGerald's *Omar*."[23]

Some of her poems were not so rich. She tried the currently popular dialect poetry in "'Grandmither, Think Not I Forget'" and in some of her other uncollected verse. She also liked the singing simplicity of Housman and Stevenson. This, with her feeling for classical restraint, kept the poems from extremes of sentiment and decoration. As others have in other times, she occasionally decried the obscurity and exaggeration of some modern poets. Praising the poems of Miss Helen Hay in 1901, she marked the admirable features of one of the sonnets as "its melody and its restraint, its distinct lack of any sort of violence or exaggeration."[24] In later years Willa Cather was to admire Robert Frost for his simplicity,

22. *Journal*, May 16, 1897.
23. See note 7, above, pp. 199-200.
24. "In Washington," *Journal*, Mar. 3, 1901, p. 12.

April

Twilights

BY

Willa Sibert Cather

❦ MR. RICHARD G. BADGER has pleasure in announcing the immediate publication of Miss Cather's first volume of poems. Many of these have already attracted marked attention in the magazines, and others, perhaps even more notable, are here printed for the first time.

❦ The title of the collection is an especially happy one; while a number of the poems draw their inspiration from Nature, others sing of varying themes and moods, but the tone of the whole collection is like that of a beautiful April evening, when the old world is young again, and the quiet charm of the clean, wholesome air and the twilight is at once restful and invigorating. It is a little book worth while.

❦ The book is handsomely printed and bound. Antique boards $1.00.

Mail announcement sent out by the publishers in April, 1903

APRIL
TWILIGHTS

POEMS BY

Willa   Sibert   Cather

ARTI ET VERI-TATI

Boston: Richard G. Badger
The Gorham Press: 1903

The title page of the original edition

his "bare and timeless world," says Miss Sergeant. "Both were suspicious of their own emotional, singing side, and imposed on it an elegant and sober line."[25] But even before she knew him, Willa Cather had chosen a poet as far from Swinburne and Verlaine as was Robert Frost. Norman Foerster writes that once, "she said that the foremost American poet was Emerson. She may have said this in Pittsburgh, more likely in Boston, where I saw her at the Touraine Hotel, looking well dressed, self-assured, important, and gracious; a *McClure's* editor, she was then on the trail of Mary Baker Eddy."[26] Although Miss Elsie Cather thought that her sister Willa always did prefer emotional rather than philosophical poetry, the choice of Emerson is not unexpected. At the age of fifteen she had filled out a chart, giving her favorite poet as Tennyson and prose writer as Emerson.[27] Certainly the transcendental belief in the high, pure truth is omnipresent in all of Cather's work. Emerson had heard the god on the mountain of Monadnoc:

> For the world was built in order,
> And the atoms march in tune;
> Rhyme the pipe, and Time the warder,
> The sun obeys them and the moon.

He, too, had his singing side.

In form, the poetry of *April Twilights* stays with the traditional ballad stanzas, couplets in tetrameter or pentameter, sonnets, and the eight-line stanza with close rhymes. One poem ("Prairie Dawn") is in blank verse. The line is usually short, though "'Grandmither, Think Not I Forget'" and "The Night Express" are in hexameters. Although Willa Cather admired the Sapphic measures, she did not use them to any extent; "Dedicatory" suggests the Greek rhythms (as does the later "Macon Prairie"). Her poetic line is smooth but not particularly supple. There is no whiplash, and few deep modulations. But some poems are as musical as Tennyson ("Asphodel" compares very well with parts of "The Lotos-Eaters"), and "I Sought the Wood in Winter" incorporates two skillfully managed, contrasting tones for the lush frailty of summer, the hard eternal core of winter.

Something of Willa Cather's craftsmanship and intentions in her poetry can be observed in the revisions she made in the texts. A few of them here will illustrate her directions (others are given in the notes).

25. *Willa Cather: A Memoir*, p. 212.
26. Letter to Bernice Slote, Nov. 19, 1961.
27. *World of Willa Cather*, pp. 112-113.

The most drastic surgery was done on "Aftermath," and it was an exciting transformation. The first version (see the notes to the poems for the complete text) was published in the *Library* for April 7, 1900. For "Aftermath" as it was included in *April Twilights*, Willa Cather wrote a completely new section for the first nine lines and revised the tenth line slightly, leaving the last four lines as they were. The theme is generally the same in the two versions, but the approach, tone, and structure are greatly different. The first version is thin and flat, loosely organized, with many clichés and some confusions. The new poem has perfect clarity, and images that are rich, vivid, and evocative. It also has something of what later critics would call paradox, ranging a series of impossibilities ("to wring / From trodden grapes the juice drunk long ago") that are joined in the imagination by the very statement. The limp rhythms of the first poem become crisp and varied in the second. Meaning is finally shaped clearly in movement, images, and structure. One most important change is from indefinite personal narrative in the first to an emphasis on universal drama in the second poem.

Some line changes in the poems also enlarge their scope. "The lad and his lass a-lying" of "In Media Vita" as it appeared first (*Lippincott's*, May, 1901) was changed to "Lads and their sweethearts lying." "Once my mother told me how" in "The Namesake" (*Lippincott's*, April, 1902) becomes "Often have they told me how." Some are revised for greater restraint. After 1903, line 22 of "'Grandmither, Think Not I Forget'" was changed from "For mine be red wi' burnin' thirst, and he must never know" to "For mine be tremblin' wi' the wish that he must never know" (*McClure's*, April, 1909). She changed it back again in 1923.

Between 1903 and 1923, Willa Cather checked errors in prosody and diction but made few real revisions in the early poems she chose to include in *April Twilights and Other Poems*. One, however, was significant. She cut the last stanza from "Lament for Marsyas," probably because it made the poem too much like Housman's "To an Athlete Dying Young" ("He was wise who did not stay / Until hands unworthy bore / Prizes that were his before"). The first two stanzas do not really say that Marsyas was lucky in death. Another reason for the cut is structural. The third stanza breaks apart after the ninth line, and the last four lines do not develop, reverse, or parallel the theme of the first section. Minor changes were made in other poems before the 1937 edition appeared. One revision which as much as anything reveals her full control of her art is the change of "purple mists ascending" in "Prairie Dawn" to "purple shadows rising." Shadows, more than mists, are organic with the images of light that follow.

In her revisions, and in her rejections of whole poems after 1903, Willa Cather seemed to be working in small ways toward a cooler, more impersonal tone, or to make universal what had started as simply individual or particular. Another example here is that for the 1923 volume she eliminated three poems with autobiographical reference ("The Namesake," "The Night Express," "Dedicatory"). She also dropped what seemed most derivative—in addition to the cut in "Lament for Marsyas," by 1937 she had dropped "In Media Vita," the other poem most like Housman. The materials of poetry, the use, the perfecting, the definition—it was all as Harsanyi had said to Thea Kronborg, "Every artist makes himself born."

3

We are not likely to read Willa Cather's poems of 1903 without thinking of them in relation to her prose, and the larger world she was to create. That they do illuminate her total work is to their author's credit, for no writer worked more than she for the principle of organic wholeness. Sometimes it came in ways she did not choose. Many elements of relationship can be found in the poems, among them a fact of literary biography: these first poems, like some of the stories which followed in the next five or six years, mark a stage in which refinement and restrained form weighed heavily against her fundamental belief in energy and emotion. Yet some of the most characteristic and creative elements of Willa Cather's later work are strongly present in the poems—the ballad tone, for example, which turned into the rougher folk language and manner of her later poetry and early novels. The most important relationships to consider in the poetry are, I think, the following: first, the early idealization of the old world; second, the symbolic significance of music; and third, incremental repetition as a creative process in her work. The first two, in particular, are brought out better in the clear focus of the poems than anywhere else.

There is always in Willa Cather's work the sense of the rare, the beautiful, the splendid thing that is a little beyond the ordinary reach—like the note too high for the human ear. It may be captured by the instrument of art; it must be sought by desire, even odysseys of heroic effort; it was, she thought in those early years, to be found only as one reached the climates nearer to the established sources of art. *April Twilights* is turned then to Europe, to the east to which she was moving, to the old south from which she came—anywhere but to Nebraska and the West. Nothing is clearer from the poems in *April Twilights* than this almost complete orientation to the ideal of some other world. But it was the young Europe that she really meant, the April time of childhood and the youth of the world; for she had first caught through the classics the sense of glory and high adventure possible to man. Such glory came from Greece and Rome, the habitation of the gods. Splendor also shone from the medieval-romantic world of cloister, sword, and lute. So most of the poems go back, as one would search a river toward the pure water of its source.

A comment Willa Cather made twenty years after *April Twilights* suggests another association she had held in her imagination. Writing of Nebraska in the *Nation*, she said: "In this newest part of the New World autumn is the season of beauty and sentiment, as spring is in the Old World."[28] Paradoxically, then, spring signified the beauty of the old and far away, autumn the beauty of the new and far too close (and readers of Willa Cather will find very few, or very brief, spring scenes in her novels; important scenes are in autumn or winter). No wonder that April enchantments were tenuous and bittersweet: they were part of that other beauty one did not have.

Although Willa Cather was writing short stories about the West at this time ("On the Divide" [1896], "Eric Hermannson's Soul" [1900], "'A Death in the Desert'" [1903]), she used the materials of her own immediate past only to dramatize the lack of that greater thing which, in her poems, hung somewhere in the bodiless world of the imagined Arcady. Other influences were of course moving like a ground swell beneath her, but at this time she could not see all ways. And here the poems are valuable as directions to the positive thing she had in view, just as the early stories show predominately the negations. I suspect that Cather's early interest in the pioneers of Nebraska was not because they came *to* the new land but because they had come *from* the old. They held the culture of that other world. In the Virginia of 1752, she wrote in the 1896 story, "A Night at Greenway Court," the very appearance of strangers "spoke to us of an older world beyond the seas for which the hearts of all of us still hungered."[29] So it was in Nebraska a century later. "The early

28. "Nebraska: The End of the First Cycle," *Nation*, CXVII (Sept. 5, 1923), 236-238.
29. *CSF*, p. 484. First published in *Nebraska Literary Magazine*, June, 1896.

population of Nebraska was largely transatlantic," she wrote in the same *Nation* article, and she stressed the value and beauty of the character and older traditions of those people. Sometimes "Cultivated, restless young men from Europe made incongruous figures among the hard-handed breakers of the soil." Literally, the world was there before her, but in her vision it was filled with those who *had* played their violins in Vienna or Prague.

The poems of *April Twilights* also show how strong in Willa Cather's imagination and habitual imagery was the archetypal figure of Apollo, god of the life-giving sun, of music and beauty. His mythic song is here the sign of creation, the invocation of magic, the perfection of beauty. In the poems, Apollo, with harp, lyre, lute, or pipe, often appears in the guise of minstrels, or shepherds, or troubadours. He is served at Delphi, the "House of Song," is the "golden harper" of "Thine Advocate," the troubadour with harpstrings in "Song," the piper of "The Encore," the rhymers of "The Tavern." His broken notes are in "Arcadian Winter," an azure song in "Sleep, Minstrel, Sleep." In "Paradox," melody is combined with youth and desire, as in so many of Cather's young artists. The music of Apollo (or Orpheus, or Marsyas) is the pure and traditional symbol for the creative desire of art.

And so we can recognize the obsession with music that runs through the Cather stories and novels, heavily at first and then more lightly as she goes farther away from the direct use of the symbol. For music continues to be the Apollonian sign of that rare and spiritual thing that art may discover. The clear statement of its symbolism is in an early story, "Eric Hermannson's Soul": "In the great world beauty comes to men in many guises, and art in a hundred forms, but for Eric there was only his violin. It stood, to him, for all the manifestations of art; it was his only bridge into the kingdom of the soul."[30]

In later works the symbol of music need not be explained; it simply

---

30. *CSF*, p. 361. First published in *Cosmopolitan*, April, 1900. Willa Cather's concept of the relationship of music and the soul (and the associated elements of harmony and order in poetry) may be clarified by a passage from a book which had been in her possession, probably during her high school years. The book, inscribed with her name but originally belonging to her high school teacher J. F. Curran, is Thomas C. Upham's *Abridgment of Mental Philosophy* (New York: Harper & Brothers, 1873). The first chapter, "Origin of Knowledge in General," includes the following: "The soul, considered in its relationship to external nature, may be compared to a stringed instrument. Regarded in itself, it is an invisible existence, having the capacity and elements of harmony. The nerves, the eye, and the senses generally, are the chords and artificial framework which God has woven round its unseen and unsearchable essence. This living and curious instrument, made up of the

functions. Its richest use is, of course, in *The Song of the Lark*,[31] the story of the creation of an artist. The young Thea Kronborg begins her real encounter with art in music of mythic significance—Gluck's *Orpheus*. She is involved in the primitive, intuitive force of art when, singing one evening with Spanish Johnny and his Mexican friends, music becomes the natural instrument of feeling. Finally the focus of the novel changes. We are no longer with Thea, but we observe her through the eyes of her old friend Dr. Archie. To him, hearing the mature operatic star Kronborg is like dreaming on a river of sound. There he seems to be looking "through an exalted calmness at a beautiful woman from far away" (500). Kronborg the artist is something other than Thea the woman. She has become the realization of art, the true song of Apollo.

To Willa Cather music meant primarily what it signified, as can be seen in her own dramatic rather than intellectual relationship with it. Her experiences in music were emotional and imaginative, Edith Lewis points out, the music "translating itself into parallel movements of thought and feeling."[32] Willa Cather recognized this in herself, as some of her comments before 1903 reveal. She wrote in the *Courier* during the winter of 1897–1898: "My friend Toby Rex [Dr. Julius Tyndale, Lincoln music and drama critic] has always accused me of too great a tendency to interpret musical compositions into literal pictures, and of caring more for the picture than for the composition in itself." For example, some weeks earlier she had described Dvorak's "Largo" from the *New World Symphony* as meaning the "empty, hungry plains of the middle west. Limitless prairies, full of the peasantry of all the nations of Europe." It was a "song of homesickness, the exile song of many nations."[33] In *The Song of the Lark* the picture became "the reaching and reaching of high plains, the immeasurable yearning of all flat lands" (251).

---

invisible soul and the bodily framework which surrounds it, is at first voiceless and silent. Nor does it appear that it will ever send forth its sounds of harmony, until it is touched and operated upon by those outward influences which exist in the various forms and adaptations of the material world. Under these influences it is first awakened into activity" (pp. 18-19).

31. Quotations from Willa Cather's novels will be cited with pagination in parentheses in the text, referring to the following editions: *The Song of the Lark* (Boston: Houghton Mifflin Company, 1937); *Alexander's Bridge* (Boston and New York: Houghton Mifflin Company, 1912); *O Pioneers!* (Boston and New York: Houghton Mifflin Company, 1913); *My Ántonia* (Boston and New York: Houghton Mifflin Company, 1918); *One of Ours* (New York: Alfred A. Knopf, 1922); *Lucy Gayheart* (New York: Alfred A. Knopf, 1961).

32. *Willa Cather Living* (New York: Alfred A. Knopf, 1953), pp. 47-48.

33. *Courier*, Feb. 5, 1898; Dec. 25, 1897.

All of this has a direct bearing on her writing. In prose, the images of music could be diffused, transformed, and enlarged. But poetry is the direct and primitive embodiment of music in language. One passage in *The Song of the Lark* shows that Cather identified the two, but that the poem might lift out of language into pure song. When Thea learns and reads the poems of *Lieder* from Professor Wunsch, her voice changes from the sound of ordinary speech as she reads "musically, like a song . . . . It was a nature-voice, Wunsch told himself, breathed from the creature and apart from language" (97). The poem itself can be Apollo's song, giving in short measure the larger design. This is what did happen in Cather's art. The poetry, especially that of 1903, forms in itself an epigraph for the novels which followed. And it makes a difference in our response to the prose works if we associate them with the poems and the god in Arcadia— to know that what has engrossed us in the novels with a sense of hidden power is that we are involved in the re-enactment of myth.

One pleasure in viewing the whole work of a writer (if he is an artist) is to recognize the accumulated complexity and richness that may develop from single first notes or chords. It is somehow satisfying to see that in the artist the large designs come out of the truth of his being. For example, we find in the poems, along with the pastoral scenes, a recurring metaphor of houses and rooms that will be enlarged into the symbolic structures of *The Professor's House* (1925).[34] In Ludlow Castle, there are the halls of vanished pleasure, the hold of power, the crypt of forgotten faith. "In Rose Time" tells that sorrow is a stone house and pleasure a straw thatch. The "House of Song" is stilled in the winter of Delphi. One poem says, "I Have No House for Love to Shelter Him" ("this darkened chamber is a house of prayer"). "The Tavern" is also the house of the heart, with verses written on the walls; the injunction is to "Tread the fire, and bar the door." In "Paradox" and "Song," the speaker is in "my tower." And the scene of "L'Envoi," like that of the Professor in his old study, is in the room of the self, "When once we are alone, and shut the door."

Other recurring themes are more incremental. The most significant, perhaps, is that of island and river as the center of the imaginative joy and dreaming expectancy of youth, a theme which expands to become river and rock. The poem "Dedicatory" states the theme in the briefest form—

34. E. K. Brown's excellent analysis of the symbolism of houses in *The Professor's House* is in his *Willa Cather: A Critical Biography*, completed by Leon Edel (New York: Alfred A. Knopf, 1953), pp. 240-246.

three children who planned "at moonrise, / On an island in a western river, / Of the conquest of the world together." The poem is paralleled by the story, "The Treasure of Far Island," which recalls the sandbar in a Nebraska river, "an enchanted river flowing peacefully out of Arcady with the Happy Isles somewhere in the distance." It was a childhood wonderland and the center of their loftiest ambitions and delightful imaginings ("'it was really our childhood that we buried here,'" says one of the characters). And the sandbar was surrounded "with all the mystery and enchantment which was attributed to certain islands of the sea by the mariners of Greece." Found again by Douglass Burnham and Margie Van Dyck, the island has the old enchantment: "out of the east rose the same moon that has glorified all the romances of the world,—that lighted Paris over the blue Aegean." The two on the island "had become as the gods, who dwell in their golden houses."[35]

The simple childhood scene of "Dedicatory" and "The Treasure of Far Island" is recalled by moments in the later novels: Bartley Alexander (*Alexander's Bridge*, 1912), going to his doomed bridge in Canada, sees from the train a group of boys around a fire and recalls "a campfire on a sandbar in a Western river" (146). An episode in *O Pioneers!* (1913)—a picnic with her brother Emil by the river—is one of the happiest days of Alexandra Bergson's life (204-205), and in *My Ántonia* (1918) the "hired girls" and Jim Burden have another picnic by a river, whose sandbars were "a sort of No Man's Land, little newly-created worlds that belonged to the Black Hawk boys" (264-279). *One of Ours* (1922) early uses a similar scene, when Claude Wheeler and his friend Ernest Havel rest and talk "on a little sandy bottom half enclosed by a loop of the creek which curved like a horseshoe" (10-11). This kind of scene is identified with preludes, with the dream of adventure and glory, with both expectation and memory.

But another element is added through a link with the poem "Paradox." In "The Treasure of Far Island," there is a specific allusion to *The Tempest*, and to Miranda on Prospero's enchanted isle: the girl in the story is once called Miranda and asked to step upon her island. Thus "Paradox," in which the speaker is on "Miranda's isle, / Which is of youth a sea-bound seigniory," is also a symbolic extension of the childhood scene; and its theme of the first creative impulse of art (or "song") is related to the image of the water-island. With both image and theme in mind, we can feel stronger overtones in that first skating scene in *Lucy Gayheart*

35. *CSF*, pp. 276-277, 280, 282. First published in *New England Magazine*, Oct., 1902.

(1935), when Lucy and Harry Gordon pause to rest on the end of an island in the Platte River. They are caught for a moment in the red sunset, "in a stream of blinding light. . . . Their faces became so brilliant that they looked at each other and laughed." Going home on the sleigh (and knowing that she is to return the next night to her music in Chicago), Lucy salutes a star with the quick joy of recognizing some eternal thing (9-12). "Star-grasping youth" is the phrase in "Paradox."

"Dedicatory" was earlier developed in a more complete parallel in the story "The Enchanted Bluff." Here the rock is added to the river image and Odysseus becomes Coronado. Six boys gathered on their sandbar dream of reaching a mysterious, storied bluff in the Southwest, the Mesa Encantada. Yet years later, returning to the Nebraska town, the narrator finds that none of the boys has found the enchanted bluff.[36] The full use of river, island, and rock is of course in Tom Outland's story in *The Professor's House*—the mesa which does contain the silent city of a lost civilization. That the rock is a transmutation of the island itself is suggested by having it encircled by the river, which must be crossed in order to reach the mesa. And going back again—the Southwest river, like curving Lovely Creek in *One of Ours*, may have come not only from the winding rivers and creeks Willa Cather knew near Red Cloud but from that other world so vivid to her, Virgil's *Georgics*. Following the assertion of the poet that he will win glory by bringing the Muse of Song to his country, Virgil literally joins the symbols of winding river and the "house of song" that Cather was to work so deeply:

> And there in the green meadows I'll build a shrine of marble
> Close to the waterside, where the river Mincius wanders
> With lazy loops and fringes the banks with delicate reed.
>
> (III, 13-15)

On the doors of Virgil's temple of art will be engraved battle scenes, and monuments will show the mythic past, including "Apollo, founder of Troy." Only with "Dedicatory" and "The Treasure of Far Island," then, do we have the full design which circles from Nebraska prairies through the Aegean world of Greek heroic adventure ("the Odysseys of summer mornings") to the Southwest desert and the heroic American past, in itself an odyssey of art.

36. *CSF*, pp. 69-77. First published in *Harper's*, April, 1909. Edith Lewis, in *Willa Cather Living*, mentions the relationship of the campfire scene in "The Enchanted Bluff" with others in *Alexander's Bridge* and *My Ántonia*, culminating in *Death Comes for the Archbishop*, as a development like that of "Vinteuil's 'little phrase'" in Proust (pp. 78-79).

The theme of adventure and elegy—the going out and the coming back—is particularly developed in "The Namesake" and "The Night Express," and their recapitulations in her later work: in a story also called "The Namesake," and in "The Sculptor's Funeral." The narrator of the story "The Namesake" (curiously, also a sculptor), tells of the making of his greatest statue, "The Color Sergeant." He had found in his grandfather's house in Pennsylvania the objects which recreated for him, on a new level of awareness, the living personality of his uncle and namesake, killed in the War between the States. For the first time he had felt "the pull of race and kindred," the union of himself with the past and the earth, which rooted him so that he received its essence even as his life seemed pouring out and running into the ground. (For this image, see also the poem "Antinous.") From "The Night Express," the dead, returning boy who had gone from home into the world becomes in "The Sculptor's Funeral" an artist who is brought back to his unappreciative home town. The scene on the station platform is the same. In the poem,

> From out the mist-clad meadows, along the river shore.
> The night express-train whistles with eye of fire before.

The story expands: "The night express shot, red as a rocket, from out the eastward marsh lands and wound along the river shore under the long lines of shivering poplars that sentineled the meadows." In both poem and story the train's whistle is the call to adventure. In the story it is called a trumpet.[37]

The theme of both these poems and the stories that developed from them is again the Virgilian "Optima dies . . . prima fugit," the elegiac strain of lost Aprils that runs so strongly in Cather's work. The dead uncle in Virginia and the dead youth in the night express are joined by Marsyas and Antinous from the poems (and some of the lost minstrels and runners); by those of talent who had died young—Keats and Chatterton, Ethelbert Nevin and Stephen Crane; by the characters in her fiction, like Tom Outland, Lucy Gayheart, and Claude Wheeler, whose great adventure to the war is to find the "something splendid" in life he had always believed was there (103). *One of Ours* is better understood when the poem "The Namesake" is read along with it. The wooers of the grave, as Cather wrote in *O Pioneers!*, are among "the young, the passionate, the gallant-hearted" (257). Still, in the war episodes of *One of*

37. *CSF*, p. 146, 174. "The Namesake" first published in *McClure's*, Mar., 1907; "The Sculptor's Funeral," *McClure's*, Jan., 1905, and in *The Troll Garden*, 1905.

Ours, David Gerhardt (the musician-soldier who had smashed his violin) says to Claude that perhaps the young men have to die "to bring a new idea into the world . . . something Olympian" (409).

These three poems—"Dedicatory," "The Namesake," and "The Night Express"—so peculiarly organic to the major themes of Cather's work, were among those she did not reprint. No doubt she looked on them as only the early sketches for what she would later develop in full. I would see them, rather, as the first lines of ballads through which incremental repetition makes the ending rich with all that has gone before.

April Twilights of 1903 marks the virtual end of Willa Cather's writing of poetry; by the revised volume of 1933 she had added only thirteen new poems to her collection. Still, it must be recorded that as early as 1912 she had had considerable recognition as a poet. Her poems were beginning to go into anthologies (see the Bibliography for "In Media Vita," "'Grandmither, Think Not I Forget,'" "L'Envoi"), and that year Albert Bigelow Paine's *Mark Twain: A Biography* included Twain's very flattering approval of her poem "The Palatine," reprinting three stanzas of it. This recognition and encouragement meant a great deal to a young writer, she said some years afterward.[38] But at that time, too, she had begun the novels which were to have her special mark.

In some ways we could almost say that Willa Cather's poems—the ones she wrote by 1903—*became* her novels. What happened to the mythic landscape of *April Twilights*? For one thing, with a certain distance of time and experience, she had turned about and found Arcadia in her own West. If Old Romance had been reality, it was finally equated by the new romance of the ordinary, transformed through the imagination.[39] She put it all in, beginning with *O Pioneers!*—the cyclic seasons and the creative

38. In a letter to Cyril Clemens (Dec. 28, 1935), a copy of which was given by Mr. Clemens to the Willa Cather Pioneer Memorial, Red Cloud, Nebraska.

39. Willa Cather's description of this change is in a statement of 1931. Explaining to an interviewer, Alice Booth ("America's Twelve Greatest Women," *Good Housekeeping,* Sept., 1931, pp. 34, 196), the difference between her early fiction and her later books, she compared the old man in the 1892 story "Peter" with his later use as Mr. Shimerda in *My Ántonia:* "In those days . . . I was afraid that people, just as they were, were not quite good enough. I felt I had to 'prettify' them. I had just heard Bernhardt and the magic of her voice was still in my ears—and so I made my old man [in "Peter"] a violinist—a good violinist, who had once played an obligato with a great singer, when she came to the little theatre in which he was first violin in the orchestra. I made that a frill for him . . . and did not realize that old *Shimerda,* just as he was, was good enough for anybody. He was not a violinist. He was just a fiddler—and not even a very good fiddler. He did not need to be. He was enough just as he was."

earth, the fields and the farmers, the glorified simple life, the themes of music as art and inspiration. And the song of Apollo she had tried on the single pure reed of the poems became magically alive and transformed into the flowing music of her prose. (Edith Lewis calls "The Enchanted Bluff" almost "a song without words.")[40] It was as if the static film of the poems were projected through a gold light, so that all the symbols moved in living figures on some great screen. The ideal old world was replaced with the ideal new world. Spring became autumn.

Willa Cather wrote of her new novels in the same terms she had used for poetry, as something intuitive, immediate, and unmistakable. True poetry has natural, inevitable form; neither the will nor technique can create it: "A man can no more write a poem by mastering poetics than a botanist can make a rose," she had said in the article on A. E. Housman. Likewise, the novels that best caught the poetic materials of memory and emotion were done with intuitive projection. Elizabeth Shepley Sergeant recalls that Cather spoke of her final form of *O Pioneers!* (two pastorals joined) as "a sudden inner explosion and enlightenment. She had experienced it before only in the conception of a poem." She would hope for the same thing in the novels, for "the explosion seemed to bring with it the inevitable shape that is not plotted but designs itself."[41] Cather's own principal statement is in the 1922 Preface to *Alexander's Bridge*: In using one's own material, the writer begins to have less power of choice, for the work has moulded itself. He depends upon the wisdom of the intuition, not of the intellect. A year before (in an interview with Latrobe Carroll in the *Bookman*, May, 1921), she had described the writing of *O Pioneers!* as the artist's submission to his material: "I decided not to 'write' at all,— simply to give myself up to the pleasure of recapturing in memory people and places I'd forgotten." ("Poetry is retrospective," she had said in the *Journal* in 1897.) Art was thus what grew in and through the memory and emotions, making itself and the artist what they were meant to be. This is not merely the pure primitivism of unstudied song; it is rather belief in the artist's connection with some great, high thing—like the Emersonian oversoul.

To return to the poems: I like to think that without the phrase in "Dedicatory"—"the Odysseys of summer mornings"—I would not have noticed one detail of an early scene in *My Ántonia*: On the Divide, "the grass was the country as the water is the sea," and there "the red of

40. *Willa Cather Living*, p. 70.
41. *Willa Cather: A Memoir*, p. 116.

the grass made all the great prairie the colour of wine-stains" (16)....
The colour of wine-stains. In that same vanished kingdom of childhood, it
was now—all over again, and perhaps in its most beautiful telling—the
odyssey of young Jim Burden (who was Willa Cather), setting out on the
wine-dark sea.

BERNICE SLOTE

Contents

✤

CONTENTS (1903)

APRIL TWILIGHTS (1903)

DEDICATORY

To R.C.C. and C.D.C.

Somewhere, sometime, in an April twilight,
When the hills are hid in violet shadows
When meadow brooks are still and hushed for wonder,
At the ring dove's call as at a summons,
Let us gather from the world's four quarters,
Stealing from the trackless dusk like shadows,
Meet to wait the moon, and greet in silence.
When she swims above the April branches,
Rises clear of naked oak and beeches,
Sit with me beneath the snowy orchard,
Where the white moth hangs with wings entranced,
Drunken with the still perfume of blossoms.
Then, for that the moon was ours of olden,
Let it work again its old enchantment.
Let it, for an April night, transform us
From our grosser selves to happy shadows
Of the three who lay and planned at moonrise,
On an island in a western river,
Of the conquest of the world together.
Let us pour our amber wine and drink it
To the memory of our vanished kingdom,
To our days of war and ocean venture,
Brave with brigandage and sack of cities;
To the Odysseys of summer mornings,
Starry wonder-tales of nights in April.

"Grandmither, Think Not I Forget"

Grandmither, think not I forget, when I come back to town,
An' wander the old ways again an' tread them up an' down.
I never smell the clover bloom, nor see the swallows pass,
Without I mind how good ye were unto a little lass.
I never hear the winter rain a-pelting all night through,
Without I think and mind me of how cold it falls on you.
And if I come not often to your bed beneath the thyme,
Mayhap 'tis that I'd change wi' ye, and gie my bed for thine,
        Would like to sleep in thine.

I never hear the summer winds among the roses blow,
Without I wonder why it was ye loved the lassie so.
Ye gave me cakes and lollipops and pretty toys a score,—
I never thought I should come back and ask ye now for more.
Grandmither, gie me your still, white hands, that lie upon your
    breast,
For mine do beat the dark all night and never find me rest;
They grope among the shadows an' they beat the cold black air,
They go seekin' in the darkness, an' they never find him there,
        An' they never find him there.

Grandmither, gie me your sightless eyes, that I may never see
His own a-burnin' full o' love that must not shine for me.
Grandmither, gie me your peaceful lips, white as the kirkyard
    snow,
For mine be red wi' burnin' thirst, an' he must never know.
Grandmither, gie me your clay-stopped ears, that I may never
    hear
My lad a-singin' in the night when I am sick wi' fear;
A-singin' when the moonlight over a' the land is white—
Aw God! I'll up an' go to him a-singin' in the night,
        A-callin' in the night.

Grandmither, gie me your clay-cold heart that has forgot to
    ache,
For mine be fire within my breast and yet it cannot break.
It beats an' throbs forever for the things that must not be,—
An' can ye not let me creep in an' rest awhile by ye?
A little lass afeard o' dark slept by ye years agone—
Ah, she has found what night can hold 'twixt sunset an' the
    dawn!
So when I plant the rose an' rue above your grave for ye,
Ye'll know it's under rue an' rose that I would like to be,
              That I would like to be.

In Rose Time

✤

Oh this is the joy of the rose;
That it blows,
And goes.

Winter lasts a five-month
    Spring-time stays but one;
Yellow blow the rye-fields
    When the rose is done.
Pines are clad at Yuletide
    When the birch is bare,
And the holly's greenest
    In the frosty air.

Sorrow keeps a stone house
    Builded grim and gray;
Pleasure hath a straw thatch
    Hung with lanterns gay.
On her petty savings
    Niggard Prudence thrives,
Passion, ere the moonset,
    Bleeds a thousand lives.

Virtue hath a warm hearth—
    Folly's dead and drowned;
Friendship hath her own when
    Love is underground.
Ah! for me the madness
    Of the spendthrift flower,
Burning myriad sunsets
    In a single hour.

For this is the joy of the rose;
That it blows,
And goes.

Asphodel

As some pale shade in glorious battle slain,
    On beds of rue, beside the silent streams,
    Recalls outworn delights in happy dreams;
The play of oars upon the flashing main,
The speed of runners, and the swelling vein,
    And toil in pleasant upland field that teems
    With vine and gadding gourd—until he seems
To feel wan memories of the sun again
    And scent the vineyard slopes when dawn is wet,
But feels no ache within his loosened knees
    To join the runners where the course is set,
Nor smite the billows of the fruitless seas,—
    So I recall our day of passion yet,
    With sighs and tenderness, but no regret.

Mills of Montmartre

❋

Upon the hill above the town—
    The old town pale and gray—
In other days went up and down
    The country lasses gay.
Below the humming mills it shone,
    Across the fields of flowers,
The city, dreamlike, far away,—
    The island, stream and towers.

The merry mills were going,
The country winds were blowing,
And brave the miller sings;
"Bring in, bring in your yellow grain,
    My weight is never light;
(Oh tall my mill and swift her wings!)
Bring in, bring in your yellow grain
    And I will give you white.
White is my hopper for your grist,
    My mill-stones you may trust:
Bring in your harvest when you list
    And I will give you dust."

Upon the hill above the town
    They grind the corn no more;
The girls go tripping up and down
    From idle door to door.

[Montmartre, the new Latin Quarter, celebrated through the Moulin Rouge and other resorts of a similar character, was once the milling suburb of Paris. Several of the old wind mills have been converted into cafes and dance halls.]

The nights are terrible with mirth,
    The days ashamed for song;
Against the sky the crimson sails
    Turn all the night-time long.

The merry mills are going,
The country winds are blowing
And brave the miller sings:
"*Bring in, bring in your yellow grain,*
    My weight is never light;
(Oh tall my mill and swift her wings!)
Bring in, bring in your yellow grain,
    And I will give you white.
Wide is my hopper for your grist,
    My mill-stones you may trust:
Bring in your harvest when you list,
    And I will give you dust."

Arcadian Winter

❖

Woe is me to tell it thee,
Winter winds in Arcady!
Scattered is thy flock and fled
From the glades where once it fed,
And the snow lies drifted white
In the bower of our delight,
Where the beech threw gracious shade
On the cheek of boy and maid;
And the bitter blasts make roar
Through the fleshless sycamore.

White enchantment holds the spring,
Where thou once wert wont to sing,
And the cold hath cut to death
Reeds melodious of thy breath.
He, the rival of thy lyre,
Nightingale with note of fire,
Sings no more; but far away,
From the windy hill-side gray,
Calls a broken note forlorn
From an aged shepherd's horn.

Still about the fire they tell
How it long ago befell
That a shepherd maid and lad
Met and trembled and were glad;
When the swift spring waters ran,
And the wind to boy or man
Brought the aching of his sires,—
Song and love and all desires.
Ere the starry dogwoods fell
They were lovers, so they tell.

Woe is me to tell it thee,
Winter winds in Arcady!
Broken pipes and vows forgot;
Scattered flocks returning not;
Frozen brook and drifted hill;
Ashen sun and song-birds still;
Songs of summer and desire
Crooned about the winter fire;
Shepherd lads with silver hair,
Shepherd maids no longer fair.

The Hawthorn Tree

Across the shimmering meadows—
Ah, when he came to me!
In the spring time,
In the night time,
In the starlight,
Beneath the hawthorn tree.

Up from the misty marsh land—
Ah, when he climbed to me!
To my white bower,
To my sweet rest,
To my warm breast,
Beneath the hawthorn tree.

Ask of me what the birds sang,
High in the hawthorn tree;
What the breeze tells,
What the rose smells,
What the stars shine—
Not what he said to me!

Sleep, Minstrel, Sleep

❄

Sleep, minstrel, sleep; the winter wind's awake,
    And yellow April's buried deep and cold.
The wood is black, and songful things forsake
    The haunted forest when the year is old.
Above the drifted snow, the aspens quake,
    The scourging clouds the shrunken moon enfold,
Denying all that nights of summer spake
    And swearing false the summer's globe of gold.

Sleep, minstrel, sleep; in such a bitter night
    Thine azure song would seek the stars in vain;
Thy rose and roundelay the winter's spite
    Would scarcely spare—O never wake again!
These leaden skies do not thy masques invite,
    Thy sunny breath would warm not their disdain;
How shouldst thou sing to boughs with winter dight,
    Or gather marigolds in winter rain?

Sleep, minstrel, sleep; we do not grow more kind;
    Your cloak was thin, your wound was wet and deep;
More bitter breath there was than winter wind,
    And hotter tears than now thy lovers weep.
Upon the world-old breast of comfort find
    How gentle Darkness thee will gently keep.
Thou wert the summer's, and thy joy declined
    When winter winds awoke. Sleep, minstrel, sleep.

Fides, Spes

✷

Joy is come to the little
    Everywhere;
Pink to the peach and pink to the apple,
    White to the pear.
Stars are come to the dogwood,
    Astral, pale;
Mists are pink on the red-bud,
    Veil after veil.
Flutes for the feathery locusts,
    Soft as spray;
Tongues of the lovers for chestnuts, poplars,
    Babbling May.
Yellow plumes for the willows'
    Wind-blown hair;
Oak trees and sycamores only
    Comfortless, bare.
Sore from steel and the watching,
    Somber and old,—
Wooing robes for the beeches, larches,
    Splashed with gold;
Breath o' love to the lilac,
    Warm with noon.—
Great hearts cold when the little
    Beat mad so soon.
What is their faith to bear it
    Till it come,
Waiting with rain-cloud and swallow,
    Frozen, dumb?

The Tavern

In the tavern of my heart
  Many a one has sat before,
Drunk red wine and sung a stave,
  And, departing, come no more.
When the night was cold without
  And the ravens croaked of storm,
They have sat them at my hearth,
  Telling me my house was warm.

As the lute and cup went round,
  They have rhymed me well in lay;—
When the hunt was on at morn,
  Each, departing, went his way.
On the walls, in compliment,
  Some would scrawl a verse or two,
Some have hung a willow branch,
  Or a wreath of corn flowers blue.

Ah! my friend, when thou dost go,
  Leave no wreath of flowers for me;
Not pale daffodils nor rue,
  Violets nor rosemary.
Spill the wine upon the lamps,
  Tread the fire, and bar the door;
So defile the wretched place
  None will come, forevermore.

In Media Vita

Streams of the spring a-singing,
    Winds o' the May that blow,
Birds from the Southland winging,
    Buds in the grasses below.
Clouds that speed hurrying over,
    And the climbing rose by the wall,
Singing of bees in the clover,
    And the dead, under all!

Lads and their sweethearts lying
    In the cleft o' the windy hill;
Hearts that hushed of their sighing,
    Lips that are tender and still.
Stars in the purple gloaming,
    Flowers that suffuse and fall,
Twitter of bird-mates homing,
    And the dead, under all!

Herdsman abroad with his collie,
    Girls on their way to the fair,
Hot lads a-chasing their folly,
    Parsons a-praying their prayer.
Children their kites a-flying,
    Grandsires that nod by the wall,
Mothers soft lullabies sighing,
    And the dead, under all!

Antinous

✻

With attributes of gods they sculptured him,
    Hermes, Osiris, but were never wise
To lift the level, frowning brow of him
    Or dull the mortal misery in his eyes;
The scornful weariness of every limb,
    The dust begotten doubt that never dies,
Antinous, beneath thy lids, though dim,
The curling smoke of altars rose to thee,
Conjuring thee to comfort and content.
    An emperor sent his galleys wide and far
To seek thy healing for thee. Yea, and spent
    Honor and treasure and red fruits of war
    To lift thy heaviness, lest thou should'st mar
The head that was an empire's glory, bent
A little, as the heavy poppies are.
    Did the perfection of thy beauty pain
Thy limbs to bear it? Did it ache to be,
    As song hath ached in men, or passion vain?
Or lay it like some heavy robe on thee?
    Was thy sick soul drawn from thee like the rain,
Or drunk up as the dead are drunk, each hour
To feed the color of some tulip flower?

Paradox

I knew them both upon Miranda's isle,
    Which is of youth a sea-bound seigniory:
Misshapen Caliban, so seeming vile,
    And Ariel, proud prince of minstrelsy,
Who did forsake the sunset for my tower
    And like a star above my slumber burned.
The night was held in silver chains by power
    Of melody, in which all longings yearned—
Star-grasping youth in one wild strain expressed,
    Tender as dawn, insistent as the tide;
The heart of night and summer stood confessed.
    I rose aglow and flung the lattice wide—
Ah jest of art, what mockery and pang!
    Alack, it was poor Caliban who sang.

Provençal Legend

❦

On his little grave and wild,
Faustinus, the martyr child,
    Candytuft and mustards grow.
Ah, how many a June has smiled
    On the turf he lies below.

Ages gone they laid him there,
Quit of sun and wholesome air,
    Broken flesh and tortured limb;
Leaving all his faith the heir
    Of his gentle hope and him.

Yonder, under pagan skies,
Bleached by rains, the circus lies,
    Where they brought him from his play.
Comeliest his of sacrifice,
    Youth and tender April day.

"Art thou not the shepherd's son?—
There the hills thy lambkins run?—
    These the fields thy brethren keep?"
"On a higher hill than yon
    Doth my Father lead His sheep."

"Bring thy ransom, then," they say,
"Gold enough to pave the way
    From the temple to the Rhone."
When he came, upon his day,
    Slender, tremulous, alone,

Mustard flowers like these he pressed,
Golden, flame-like, to his breast,

Blooms the early weanlings eat.
When his Triumph brought him rest,
    Yellow bloom lay at his feet.

Golden play days came: the air
Called him, weanlings bleated there,
    Roman boys ran fleet with spring;
Shorn of youth and usage fair,
    Hope nor hilltop days they bring.

But the shepherd children still
Come at Easter, warm or chill,
    Come with violets gathered wild
From his sloping pasture hill,
Playfellows who would fulfil
    Playtime to that martyr child.

Winter at Delphi

❄

Cold are the stars of the night,
 Wild is the tempest crying,
Fast through the velvet dark
 Little white flakes are flying.
Still is the House of Song,
 But the fire on the hearth is burning;
And the lamps are trimmed and the cup
 Is full for his day of returning.
His watchers are fallen asleep,
 They wait but his call to follow,
Ay, to the ends of the earth—
 But Apollo, the god, Apollo?

Sick is the heart in my breast,
 Mine eyes are blinded with weeping;
The god who never comes back,
 The watch that forever is keeping.
Service of gods is hard;
 Deep lies the snow on my pillow.
For him the laurel and song,
 Weeping for me and the willow:
Empty my arms and cold
 As the nest forgot of the swallow:
Birds will come back with the spring,—
 But Apollo, the god, Apollo?

Hope will come back with the spring,
 Joy with the lark's returning;
Love must awake betimes,
 When crocus buds are a-burning.
Hawthorns will follow the snow,
 The robin his tryst be keeping;

Winds will blow in the May,
 Waking the pulses a-sleeping.
Snowdrops will whiten the hills,
 Violets hide in the hollow:
Pan will be drunken and rage—
 But Apollo, the god, Apollo?

On Cydnus

The dream of all the world was at his feet:
    Her eyes were heavy with the night of fate,
    When, from the purple couch whereon she sate,
She rose, and took a jewel that was meet
For a queen's breast, where royal pulses beat—
    A milk-white pearl, her milk-white bosom's mate,
    Dropped in the golden chalice at his plate,
And to his lips held up the nectar sweet
    And bade him drink the cup of destiny.
How shall he pledge again? by what emprise
    A chalice find that holds a kingdom's fee?
Perchance in that charmed liquor he descries
    A madman, raving while his galleys flee,
    Who casts a world into the wine-dark sea.

The Namesake

TO W. S. B., OF THE THIRTY-THIRD VIRGINIA

Vigesimum post annum in obscurum correpto lucem
vigesimi gaudens percipisse.

Two by two and three by three
Missouri lies by Tennessee;
Row on row, an hundred deep,
Maryland and Georgia sleep;
Wistfully the poplars sigh
Where Virginia's thousands lie.

Somewhere there among the stones,
All alike, that mark their bones,
Lies a lad beneath the pine
Who once bore a name like mine,—
Flung his splendid life away
Long before I saw the day.

Often have they told me how
Hair like mine grew on his brow.
He was twenty to a day
When he got his jacket gray—
He was barely twenty-one
When they found him by his gun.

Tell me, Uncle by the pine,
Had you such a girl as mine,
When you put her arms away
Riding to the wars that day?
Were her lips so cold, instead
You must needs to kiss the lead?

Had the bugle, lilting gay,
Sweeter things than she to say?
Were there no gay fellows then,
You must seek these silent men?
Was your luck so bad at play
You must game your bones away?

Ah! you lad with hair like mine,
Sleeping by the Georgia pine,
I'd be quick to quit the sun
Just to help you hold your gun,
And I'd leave my girl to share
Your still bed of glory there.

Proud it is I am to know
In my veins there still must flow,
There to burn and bite alway,
That proud blood you threw away;
And I'll be winner at the game
Enough for two who bore the name.

Lament for Marsyas

Marsyas sleeps. Oh, never wait,
Maidens, by the city gate,
Till he come to plunder gold
Of the daffodils you hold,
Or your branches white with May;
He is whiter gone than they.
He will startle you no more
When along the river shore
Damsels beat the linen clean.
Nor when maidens play at ball
Will he catch it where it fall:
Though ye wait for him and call
He will answer not, I ween.

Happy Earth to hold him so,
Still and satisfied and low,
Giving him his will—ah more
Than a woman could before!
Still forever holding up
To his parted lips the cup
Which hath eased him, when to bless
All who loved were powerless.
Ah! for that too-lovely head,
Low among the laureled dead,
Many a rose earth oweth yet;
Many a yellow jonquil brim,
Many a hyacinth dewy-dim,
For the singing breath of him
Sweeter than the violet.

Marsyas sleeps: Ah! well-a-day,
He was wise who did not stay

Until hands unworthy bore
Prizes that were his before.
Him the god hath put for long
With the elder choir of song—
They who turned them from the sun
Ere their singing days were done,
Or the lips of praise were chill.
Whether summer come or go,
April bud or winter blow,
He will never heed or know
Underneath the daffodil.

White Birch in Wyoming

❀

Stark as a Burne-Jones vision of despair,
    Amid the painted glare of sand and sky,
She stands, so naked seeming to the air,
    Where heat has drunk the living water dry.

The tender color of the verdant North,
    The waterfall and streaming mists I know,
Where, from the winding valleys trooping forth,
    Her Valkyr sisters hurry toward the snow.

Queen warrior women, silver mailed and white,
    From mountain fastnesses which they command,
Bemoan her through the starry Northern night,
    Brunhilda, girdled by the burning sand.

I Sought the Wood in Winter

I sought the wood in summer
    When every twig was green;
The rudest boughs were tender
    And buds were pink between.
Light-fingered aspens trembled
    In fitful sun and shade,
And daffodils were golden
    In every starry glade.
The brook sang like a robin—
    My hand could check him where
The lissome maiden willows
    Shook out their yellow hair.

"How frail a thing is Beauty,"
    I said, "when every breath
She gives the vagrant summer
    But swifter woos her death.
For this the star dust troubles,
    For this have ages rolled;
To deck the wood for bridal
    And slay her with the cold."

I sought the wood in winter
    When every leaf was dead;
Behind the wind-whipped branches
    The winter sun set red.
The coldest star was rising
    To greet that bitter air,
The oaks were writhen giants;
    Nor bud nor bloom was there.
The birches, white and slender,
    In deathless marble stood,

The brook, a white immortal,
    Slept silent in the wood.

"How sure a thing is Beauty,"
    I cried. "No bolt can slay,
No wave nor shock despoil her,
    No ravishers dismay.
Her warriors are the angels
    That cherish from afar,
Her warders people Heaven
    And watch from every star.
The granite hills are slighter,
    The sea more like to fail;
Behind the rose the planet,
    The Law behind the veil."

Evening Song

✤

Dear love, what thing of all the things that be
Is ever worth one thought from you or me,
    Save only Love,
    Save only Love?

The days so short, the nights so quick to flee,
The world so wide, so deep and dark the sea,
    So dark the sea;

So far the suns and every listless star,
Beyond their light—Ah! dear, who knows how far,
    Who knows how far?

One thing of all dim things I know is true,
The heart within me knows, and tells it you,
    And tells it you.

So blind is life, so long at last is sleep,
And none but Love to bid us laugh or weep,
    And none but Love,
    And none but Love.

Eurydice

A bitter doom they did upon her place:
She might not touch his hand nor see his face
The while he led her up from death and dreams
Into his world of bright Arcadian streams.
For all of him she yearned to touch and see,
Only the sweet ghost of his melody;
For all of him she yearned to have and hold,
Only the wraith of song, sweet, sweet and cold.
With only song to stop her ears by day
And hold above her frozen heart alway,
And strain within her arms and glad her sight,
With only song to feed her lips by night,
To lay within her bosom only song—
Sweetheart! the way from Hell's so long, so long!

The Encore

❖

No garlands in the winter time,
    No trumpets in the night!
The song ye praise was done lang syne,
    And was its own delight.
O' God's name take the wreath away,
    Since now the music's sped;
Ye never cry, "Long live the king!"
    Until the king is dead.

When I came piping through the land,
    One morning in the spring,
With cockle burrs upon my coat,
    'Twas then I was a king:
A mullein sceptre in my hand,
    My order daisies three,
With song's first freshness on my lips—
    And then ye pitied me!

London Roses

"Rowses, Rowses! Penny a bunch!" they tell you—
Slattern girls in Trafalgar, eager to sell you.
Roses, roses, red in the Kensington sun,
Holland Road, High Street, Bayswater, see you and
    smell you—
Roses of London town, red till the summer is done.

Roses, roses, locust and lilac, perfuming
West End, East End, wondrously budding and blooming
Out of the black earth, rubbed in a million hands,
Foot-trod, sweat-sour over and under, entombing
Highway of darkness, deep gutted with iron bands.

"Rowses, rowses! Penny a bunch!" they tell you,
Ruddy blooms of corruption, see you and smell you,
Born of stale earth, fallowed with squalor and tears—
North shire, south shire, none are like these, I tell you,
Roses of London perfumed with a thousand years.

The Night Express

✛

From out the mist-clad meadows, along the river shore,
The night express-train whistles with eye of fire before.
A trail of smoke behind her enclouds the rising moon
That gilds the sighing poplars and floods the wide lagoon.
Through yellow fields of harvest and waving fields of corn
The night express-train rumbles with whistle low and
　　lorn.
The silent village harkens the sound it knows so well,
And boys wait on the siding to hear the engine-bell,
While lads who used to loiter with wistful steps and slow,
Await to-night a comrade who comes, but will not go.
The train that brings to mothers the news of sons who
　　roam
Shoots red from out the marshes to bring a rover home.

With restless heart of boyhood we watched that head-
　　light when
The whistle seemed to call us to dare the world of men;
To leave the plow and herd-whip for lads with hearts of
　　clay,
And while our blood was leaping be up and far away;
To find the great world somewhere, to wander wide and
　　see
If men of coast or mountain were better men than we.
We heard the hoarse throat whistle, we heard the engine-
　　bell,
We saw the red eye blazing, we knew the hot heart well.
But little could we reckon, gay-hearted boys at play,
The horse that took us out to men would bring us home
　　one day;
That took us out at morning, with shining wheels ahum,
Would bring us home at evening, when we are glad to
　　come.

Ah! let my fight be fiercer, the little time before
They bring me still and weary along the river shore.
Then may the wheels turn swiftly behind the eye of fire,
And may the bell ring gaily that brings me my desire.
The boys I used to watch with will all be there to see,
When I come home to rest me in the ground that
    nurtured me.
To earth I digged in boyhood, through fields I used to
    keep,
The lads who wrought beside me shall bear me home to
    sleep.
From out the mist-clad marshes, along the river shore,
With trail of smoke behind me and eye of fire before;
And youths will watch with burning to seek the world of
    men,
And thrill to hear the whistle that brings me home again.

Prairie Dawn

A crimson fire that vanquishes the stars;
A pungent odor from the dusty sage;
A sudden stirring of the huddled herds;
A breaking of the distant table-lands
Through purple mists ascending, and the flare
Of water ditches silver in the light;
A swift, bright lance hurled low across the world;
A sudden sickness for the hills of home.

Aftermath

Can'st thou conjure a vanished morn of spring,
　　Or bid the ashes of the sunset glow
Again to redness? Are we strong to wring
　　From trodden grapes the juice drunk long ago?
Can leafy longings stir in Autumn's blood,
　　Or can I wear a pearl dissolved in wine,
Or go a-Maying in a winter wood,
　　Or paint with youth thy wasted cheek, or mine?
What bloom, then, shall abide, since ours hath sped?
　　Thou art more lost to me than they who dwell
In Egypt's sepulchres, long ages fled;
　　And would I touch—Ah me! I might as well
Covet the gold of Helen's vanished head,
　　Or kiss back Cleopatra from the dead!

Thine Advocate

*

When this swarth body, in revolt and pain,
　　Erreth against thy love's sweet majesty,
　　Doing thee wrong that is more wrong to me,
And from its dearest usage would refrain,
And soweth hate where our clasped hands have lain
　　And discord where accord was wont to be,—
　　Turning thy breath to bitterness in thee,
Which, doubly bitter, stingeth me again,—
　　My golden harper, sickened of the sun,
Wild-eyed and tearful through his wind-blown hair,
　　The psalmist of thy beauty, who is one
With it, then fleeth up his narrow stair
　　And weepeth for thee till the stars are come,
　　As David sometime mourned for Absalom.

*Poppies on Ludlow Castle**

❖

Through halls of vanished pleasure,
    And hold of vanished power,
And crypt of faith forgotten,
    I came to Ludlow tower.

A-top of arch and stairway,
    Of crypt, and donjon cell,
Of council hall, and chamber,
    Of wall, and ditch, and well.

High over grated turrets
    Where clinging ivies run,
A thousand scarlet poppies
    Enticed the rising sun.

Upon the topmost tower,
    With death and damp below,—
Three hundred years of spoilage,—
    The crimson poppies grow.

—This hall it was that bred him,
    These hills that knew him brave,
The gentlest English singer
    That fills an English grave.—

How have they heart to blossom
    So cruel gay and red,
When beauty so hath perished
    And valor so hath sped?

*Ludlow Castle, in Shropshire, was the seat where Sir Philip Sidney spent a part of his youth, when his father was governor of the Welsh border.

When knights so fair are rotten,
 And captains true asleep,
And singing lips are dust-stopped
 Six English earth-feet deep?

When ages old remind me
 How much hath gone for naught,
What wretched ghost remaineth
 Of all that flesh hath wrought;

Of love and song and warring,
 Of adventure and play,
Of art and comely building,
 Of faith and form and fray,

I'll mind the flowers of pleasure,
 Of short-lived youth and sleep,
That drank the sunny weather
 A-top of Ludlow keep.

Sonnet

Alas, that June should come when thou didst go;
I think you passed each other on the way;
And seeing thee, the Summer loved thee so
That all her loveliness she gave away;
Her rare perfumes, in hawthorn boughs distilled,
Blushing, she in thy sweeter bosom left,
Thine arms with all her virgin roses filled,
Yet felt herself the richer for thy theft;
Beggared herself of morning for thine eyes,
Hung on the lips of every bird the tune,
Breathed on thy cheek her soft vermilion dyes,
And in thee set the singing heart of June.
And so, not only do I mourn thy flight,
But Summer comes despoiled of her delight.

Thou Art the Pearl

I read of knights who laid their armor down,
    And left the tourney's prize for other hands,
And clad them in a pilgrim's somber gown,
    To seek a holy cup in desert lands.
For them no more the torch of victory;
    For them lone vigils and the starlight pale,
So they in dreams the Blessed Cup may see—
            Thou art the Grail!

An Eastern king once smelled a rose in sleep,
    And on the morrow laid his scepter down.
His heir his titles and his lands might keep,—
    The rose was sweeter wearing than the crown.
Nor cared he that its life was but an hour,
    A breath that from the crimson summer blows,
Who gladly paid a kingdom for a flower—
            Thou art the Rose!

A merchant man, who knew the worth of things,
    Beheld a pearl more priceless than a star;
And straight returning, all he hath he brings
    And goes upon his way, Ah, richer far!
Laughter of merchants of the market place,
    Nor taunting gibe nor scornful lips that curl,
Can ever cloud the rapture on his face—
            Thou art the Pearl!

From the Valley

Toward the heights the pines climb row on row,
Processional guardians of the vestal snow,
Steel clad and somber, with their lances set
Against my heart, and like an old regret
For life unlived and love that could not be
Fall darkness, and the mountain's mystery.
Between the peaks, with line inviolate,
The arc of some vast wreck of Titan state
Yawns wide and cold, and empty galleries lie
Reverberating silence like a cry.
From ledges lifting skyward, tier on tier,
The elder gods, implacable, austere,
In their imperishable seats and high,
Behold the valley where our days go by
Like shining water, coming not again.
The solemn ministries of love and pain,
The runner fallen and the strong brought low,
And hands bound hard by sins of long ago.
But when the pines to twilight stars complain,
They drop the misty curtains of the rain,—
Whether from pity we can never know,
Or languor at the dullness of the show.

I Have No House for Love to Shelter Him

❖

Since thou came'st not at morn, come not at even;
  Let night close peaceful where it hath begun.
Affrighten not the restful stars from heaven
  With futile after-glimpses of the sun.
My heart inclines me, but my lands are wasted,
  My treasure spent, and evening closes dim;
Spring's fair demesne the chilling frost hath tasted—
  I have no house for Love to shelter him.

No raiment fair to clothe his limbs so tender;
  No spicèd wines to cool his burning lip;
No garlands wherewithal to crown his splendor;
  No lute to tune to songful fellowship.
No pillow for the twilights of his dreaming;
  No roses on these brows, with winter grim,
Wherewith to strew his couch, as were beseeming—
  I have no house for Love to shelter him.

Ride on, and tarry not, O kingly stranger!
  This darkened chamber is a house of prayer;
A place of vigils, and to youth a danger—
  'Twas fair at morning, but thou wert not there.
Who woos the sapless winter for his lover,
  Or hangs his garlands at a cloister grim?
Oh! bid me not my nakedness discover,—
  I have no house for Love to shelter him!

The Poor Minstrel

Does the darkness cradle thee
Than mine arms more tenderly?
Do the angels God hath put
　　There to guard thy lonely sleep—
One at head and one at foot—
　　Watch more fond and constant keep?
When the black-bird sings in May,
　　And the Spring is in the wood,
Would you never trudge the way
　　Over hilltops, if you could?
Was my harp so hard a load
　　Even on the sunny morns
When the plumèd huntsmen rode
　　To the music of their horns?
Hath the love that lit the stars,
　　Fills the sea and moulds the flowers,
Whose completeness nothing mars,
　　Made forgot what once was ours?
Christ hath perfect rest to give;
　　Stillness and perpetual peace;
You, who found it hard to live,
　　Sleep and sleep, without surcease.

Christ hath stars to light thy porch,
　　Silence after fevered song;—
I had but a minstrel's torch
　　And the way was wet and long.
Sleep. No more on winter nights,
　　Harping at some castle gate,
Thou must see the revel lights
　　Stream upon our cold estate.
Bitter was the bread of song

While you tarried in my tent,
And the jeering of the throng
    Hurt you, as it came and went.
When you slept upon my breast
    Grief had wed me long ago:
Christ hath his perpetual rest
    For thy weariness. But Oh!
When I sleep beside the road,
    Thanking God thou liest not so,
Brother to the owl and toad,
    Could'st thou, Dear, but let me know,
Does the darkness cradle thee
Than mine arms more tenderly?

Paris

Behind the arch of glory sets the day;
The river lies in curves of silver light,
The Fields Elysian glitter in a spray
Of golden dust; the gilded dome is bright,
The towers of Notre Dame cut clean and gray
The evening sky, and pale from left to right
A hundred bridges leap from either quay.
Pillared with pride, the city of delight
Sits like an empress by her silver Seine,
Heavy with jewels, all her splendid dower
Flashing upon her, won from shore and main
By shock of combat, sacked from town and tower.
Wherever men have builded hall or fane
Red war hath gleaned for her and men have slain
To deck her loveliness. I feel again
That joy which brings her art to faultless flower,
That passion of her kings, who, reign on reign,
Arrayed her star by star with pride and power.

Song

Troubadour, when you were gay,
You wooed with rose and roundelay,
Singing harpstrings, sweet as May.
From beneath the crown of bay
Fell the wild, abundant hair.
Scent of cherry bloom and pear
With you from the south did fare,
Buds of myrtle for your wear.
Soft as summer stars thine eyes,
Planets pale in violet skies;
Summer wind that sings and dies
Was the music of thy sighs.

Troubadour, one winter's night,
When the pasture lands were white
And the cruel stars were bright,
Fortune held thee in despite.
Then beneath my tower you bore
Rose nor rondel as of yore,
But a heavy grief and sore
Laid in silence at my door.
April yearneth, April goes;
Not for me her violet blows,
I have done for long with those.
At my breast thy sorrow grows,
Nearer to my heart, God knows,
Than ever roundelay or rose!

L'Envoi

Where are the loves that we have loved before
When once we are alone, and shut the door?
No matter whose the arms that held me fast,
The arms of Darkness hold me at the last.
No matter down what primrose path I tend,
I kiss the lips of Silence in the end.
No matter on what heart I found delight,
I come again unto the breast of Night.
No matter when or how love did befall,
'Tis Loneliness that loves me best of all,
And in the end she claims me, and I know
That she will stay, though all the rest may go.
No matter whose the eyes that I would keep
Near in the dark, 'tis in the eyes of Sleep
That I must look and look forever more,
When once I am alone, and shut the door.

Notes on the Poems of April Twilights

❈

Typographical and orthographical errors in the 1903 printing of *April Twilights* have been corrected by the editor in the present edition as follows: "'Grandmither, Think Not I Forget,'" l. 18—"As They" (*1903*) changed to "An' they"; "Antinous," l. 13—"least" (*1903*) changed to "lest"; "Paradox," l. 10—"insistant" (*1903*) changed to "insistent"; "On Cydnus," title in both text and table of contents—corrected from "On Cyndus"; "Lament for Marsyas," l. 26—"dewey" (*1903*) changed to "dewy"; "I Sought the Wood in Winter," l. 34—"I cried," (*1903*) changed to "I cried."; "The Night Express," l. 33—"mist clad" (*1903*) changed to "mist-clad" in accordance with l. 1 and the first printing in *Youth's Companion* (1902); "Thine Advocate," l. 14—"Absolom" (*1903*) changed to "Absalom"; "Poppies on Ludlow Castle," l. 10—"ivys" (*1903*) changed to "ivies"; "I Have No House for Love to Shelter Him," l. 7—"demense" (*1903*) changed to "demesne," and l. 10— "spicéd" changed to "spicèd"; "The Poor Minstrel," l. 13—"pluméd" (*1903*) changed to "plumèd"; "Song," ll. 1 and 13—"Troubador" (*1903*) changed to "Troubadour."

Some revisions and editorial changes were made in the poems of *April Twilights* as they appeared in magazines and newspapers and in three editions, here abbreviated as *1903*, *1923*, and *1937*. (See the Bibliography, pp. 75–88, for complete references.) In the following notes, only significant revisions are cited. Purely stylistic differences in punctuation, hyphenation, and spelling are not indicated.

DEDICATORY

The island here referred to is in the Republican River, near Red Cloud, Nebraska. It is described in Willa Cather's story "The Treasure of Far Island" (*CSF*, pp. 265–282; first published in *New England Magazine*, Oct., 1902):

Far Island is an oval sand bar, half a mile in length and perhaps a hundred yards wide, which lies about two miles up from Empire City in a turbid little Nebraska river. The island is known chiefly to the children who dwell in that region, and generation after generation of them have claimed it; fished there, and pitched their tents under the great arched tree, and built camp fires on its level, sandy outskirts. In the middle of the island, which is always above water except in flood time, grow thousands of yellow-green willows and cottonwood seedlings, brilliantly green, even when the hottest winds blow, by reason of the surrounding moisture. In the summer months, when the capricious stream is low, the children's empire is extended by many rods, and a long irregular beach of white sand is exposed along the east coast of the island, never out of the water long enough to acquire any vegetation, but dazzling white, ripple marked, and full of possibilities for the imagination.

"GRANDMITHER, THINK NOT I FORGET"

In the printings before 1903 and in *McClure's* (1909), l. 33 read "An' she has found." Other variations found only in the *McClure's* version and its reprinting in *Current Literature*: l. 12 read "store" instead of "score." The first word of l. 18 was omitted, reading "They never find him there." Two other line changes were made in *McClure's*: l. 22 became "For mine be tremblin' wi' the wish that he must never know," and l. 30 became "Wi' every beat it's callin' for things that must not be,—" l. 26 read "Ah, God!" instead of "Aw God!" *1923* is in general like *1903*, but in *1937* l. 28 reads "clay-clod" instead of "clay-cold."

IN ROSE TIME

The first printing in *Lippincott's* (1902) had "five-months" instead of "five-month" (l. 4) and "heart" instead of "hearth" (l. 20). In both *1923* and *1937* the title is hyphenated ("In Rose-Time") and colons are placed after "rose" in ll. 1 and 28.

ARCADIAN WINTER

In all printings other than *1903*, commas are used instead of semicolons at the ends of lines. In *1923* and *1937*, ll. 19-20 read "the broken note forlorn / Of" instead of "a broken note forlorn / From."

SLEEP, MINSTREL, SLEEP

The title is placed in quotation marks in *1923* and *1937*, and l. 6 reads "a shrunken" instead of "the shrunken." In *1937*, "thy" in l. 20 is changed to "your."

FIDES, SPES

In the later printings in *McClure's* (1909) and in *1923* and *1937*, l. 11 reads "Tongues of lovers" instead of "Tongues of the lovers," and ll. 19-22 are enclosed in parentheses rather than dashes. Line 21 is revised in *1923* and *1937*, with "of love" instead of "o' love" and "lilacs" instead of "lilac."

THE TAVERN

In both *1923* and *1937*, "defile" in l. 23 has been changed to "despoil," perhaps at the suggestion of the reviewer in the New York *Times Saturday Review* (June 20, 1903). However, see also Willa Cather's other uses of "despoil" in "I Sought the Wood in Winter" and "Sonnet."

IN MEDIA VITA

In the first printing in *Lippincott's* (1901), a number of lines had different phrasing from that of *1903*:

	1901	1903
l. 3	"Birds of the Southland"	"Birds from the Southland"
l. 4	"And the buds in the grasses"	"Buds in the grasses"
l. 9	"The lad and his lass a-lying"	"Lads and their sweethearts lying"
l. 18	"The lass on her way"	"Girls on their way"
l. 20	"The parson a-praying"	"Parsons a-praying"

Further changes were made in *1923*: in ll. 2 and 10, the "o'" used in *1903* was made "of"; in l. 11, what may have been an omitted "are" was inserted before "hushed"; and in l. 19, "Hot lads" of the *1903* was changed to "Young lads." The poem was omitted from *1937*.

THE NAMESAKE

In the first printings (*Lippincott's* and the *Courier*, 1902) the subtitle read, "To W. L. B., of the Thirty-Fifth Virginia." This was changed in *1903* to "To W. S. B., of the Thirty-Third Virginia." The uncle who was killed in the Civil War was William Sibert Boak. "W. L. B." could refer only to Willa Cather's maternal grandfather, William Lee Boak, and like the "Thirty-Fifth" was clearly an error that was corrected in *1903*. Only indirectly was Willa Cather named for either of the Williams. The name on her birth certificate was "Wilella" (for an aunt who had died in childhood), but she was called "Willie" or "Willa," and she herself changed the name in the family Bible to

"Willa." In later years she used first "Love" and then "Sibert" as middle names. See Bennett, *The World of Willa Cather*, pp. 234-235.

The epigraph may be translated as, "After twenty years, snatched up into darkness, but glad to see the light of the twentieth."

A few other textual revisions were made for the 1903 printing:

1902	1903
l. 5 "And the wistful poplars"	"Wistfully the poplars"
l. 13 "Once my mother told me"	"Often have they told me"
l. 36 "Your six feet of glory"	"Your still bed of glory"

LAMENT FOR MARSYAS

The last stanza of the poem was omitted in both *1923* and *1937*. In *1937*, l.5 reads "Of your branches" instead of "Or your branches."

Marsyas, the celebrated piper of Phrygia, challenged Apollo to a contest of music to be judged by the Muses. The loser was to be bound to a tree and flayed to death by the winner. Marsyas lost. "The death of Marsyas was universally lamented," says Lemprière. The "Fauns, Satyrs, and Dryads wept at his fate," and from their tears arose the river Marsyas.

I SOUGHT THE WOOD IN WINTER

The title is in quotation marks in *1923* but not in *1937*. In both editions, a colon instead of a semicolon is used after "rolled" in l. 18.

THE ENCORE

In its original printing as "The Poet to His Public" (*Nebraska State Journal*, and probably "Christmas *Lippincott*," 1900), the poem had "No trumpet" instead of "No trumpets" in l. 2, and "The song of praise" instead of "The song ye praise" in l. 3.

LONDON ROSES

In the reprinting in *McClure's* (1909), l. 10 read "Highways of darkness, gutted with iron bands" instead of "Highway of darkness, deep gutted with iron bands." It was changed back to the original form in *1923* and *1937*, except that "Highways" was kept in the plural.

THE NIGHT EXPRESS

In the first printings (*Youth's Companion* and *Nebraska State Journal*, 1902) l. 12 read "to bring a wanderer home," changed in *1903* to "to bring a rover home." The *Journal* also had other variations:

"whistles" (l. 14), later revised to "whistle"; "far away" (l. 16), revised to "fare away"; "light-hearted" (l. 21), revised to "gay-hearted"; "to rest in the ground" (l. 30), revised to "to rest me in the ground."

PRAIRIE DAWN

A number of revisions were made for the 1937 edition. Among the punctuation changes is a period placed after "world" (l. 7) instead of the semicolon used previously. Line 5 reads "shadows rising" instead of "mists ascending" and "flash" instead of "flare."

AFTERMATH

The following is Version 1 of "Aftermath" as it appeared in the *Library* (April 7, 1900):

AFTERMATH

By Willa Sibert Cather

Last night I stood upon the hill awhile
 Where first I learned to love you in the spring
 When tender April woods were burgeoning.
Ah! I have felt less lonely by the Nile,
Nearer to life in some gray Grecian pile,
 Where souls of the departed poets sing
 From laurel thickets purple blossoming,
As in the silence of the cloister aisle.
 So far our little yesterday hath sped
You seem more lost to me than they who dwell
 In Egypt's sepulchres, long ages fled,
And would I touch—Ah me! I might as well
 Covet the gold of Helen's vanished head,
 Or kiss back Cleopatra from the dead!

POPPIES ON LUDLOW CASTLE

The footnote is omitted in *1923* and *1937*. In both of those editions, l. 13 reads "topmost turret" instead of "topmost tower," as it was in *1903*. The dashes have been omitted from the beginning and end of stanza five.

THE POOR MINSTREL

In the reprinting in *McClure's* (1911), rhythm is affected by some punctuation changes: commas inserted after "morns" (l. 12), "sea" (l. 16), "give" (l. 19), "Stillness" (l. 20), "torch" (l. 25), "But" (l. 38); commas omitted after "You" (l. 21) and "you" (l. 34). That these changes, as well as most of the others made in the poems reprinted in *McClure's*, were not retained in the 1923 and 1937 editions suggests that the variations in *McClure's* may not have come from Willa Cather's own editing.

Appendix

Other Verses

This selection of Willa Cather's verse includes her first published poems, a group of children's poems (most of them with personal reference to the children in her own family), and other light verse published before 1903. It omits translations, the verse used as epigraphs to stories (available in *CSF*), and other magazine verse presumably eligible for *April Twilights* in 1903 but rejected by Miss Cather.

Unsigned and pseudonymous poems are identified as Willa Cather's primarily by personal associations. "'Thine Eyes So Blue and Tender'" (Emily Vantell), "Bobby Shafto" (John Esten), and "My Horseman" (unsigned) are included in a scrapbook of Willa Cather's poems kept by her family, and the pseudonyms of "Emily Vantell" and "John Esten" (also used for "My Little Boy") can thus be affirmed. Another copy of "My Horseman" was inscribed and sent to her brother James by Willa Cather. On the copy of "Are You Sleeping, Little Brother?" in the scrapbook Willa Cather has inscribed "(Jack)" after the line "To J. E. C." and has completed the signature to make it read "W. S. Cather." (See also "A Note on Identifications" in the Bibliography.)

Although none of these poems would have been appropriate for *April Twilights*, they will have some interest as a part of Willa Cather's literary biography and, in a more personal way, suggest some new dimensions for the author herself. It should be said that from accounts of her family and friends, Willa Cather had unusual skill in composing stories and poems for children—with sometimes unusual artistry, as in the stories "The Strategy of the Were-Wolf Dog" and "The Princess Baladina" (*CSF*, 441 ff. and 567 ff.). But she was as prodigal with them as she was productive, and that phase of her writing may be hard to define. The poems which follow may be introduced by a comment she once made on Eugene Field's poems for children: not great, she said, but "quaint and tender and in their own way beautiful" (*Courier*, Nov. 9, 1895). "Buffalo Bill's Valedictory" may also be for the children, but it has in it seeds of a new western world that would eventually be created, as through the lines of "Are You Sleeping, Little Brother?" we can look ahead into Thea Kronborg's childhood in the first part of *The Song of the Lark*.

The poems which follow are printed in the order of their first appearance and with their original arrangements of titles and signatures.

SHAKESPEARE

A FRESHMAN THEME

World poet, we now of this latter day
Who have known failure and have felt defeat,
The dwarfed children of earth's sterile age,
Who feel our weakness weighing on our limbs
Unbreakable as bonds of adamant,
Turn to thee once again, O sun born bard:
To rest our weary souls a little space
Beneath the shadow of infinitude.
As weak men who have fallen very low,
Look toward high heaven and find some comfort there,
Knowing, however low themselves may fall,
The great blue reaches on, forever up.
O Mystery unsearchable! at times
We seek to find thy great soul's secret out,
And when some light streams like the setting sun
Across a watery waste, like swimmers bold
We plunge into that path of quivering gold,
And with long strokes we cleave the glowing wave
Straight toward the sun. But when its last caress
Leaves the horizon dark, about us steals
The awful horror of the open sea.
Thy mystery is great as is thy power,
And those who love thee most know only this,
As long since knew the men of Ithaca:
Within the great hall of our armory
Where hang the weapons of our ancient chiefs
And mighty men of old, there hangs a bow
Of clanging silver, which today no man,
Be he of mortal mother or the son
Of some sea goddess, can its tense drawn cord
Loosen, or bend at all its massive frame.
Beneath it hang the bronze shod shafts which none

Have cunning to in these days to fit thereto,
Above it all the sun stands still in heaven,
Pierced there long centuries with a shaft of song.

W. Cather
Hesperian, XXI (June 1, 1892), 3.

COLUMBUS

O master of all seamen and all seas,
Who first dared set a sail toward sunset shores,
Not as Odysseus sailed thou, for the love
Of blue sea water, nor of the sweet sound
Of surges smiting on thy vessel's prow;
Nor of the soft white bosom of thy sail
Swelling against blue heaven. Unto thee
The waters were but wastes that lay between
Thee and thy prize. The stars of heaven, guides
That pointed toward the ever-widening west.
Prophet wer't thou, who saw in things that were
Only the future, and thy soul was set
To journey toward the west, like kings of old
Who followed from the east a western star.
Most happy of all bards wert thou, who saw
Thy fancies take upon them form and shape
Thy realized ideal in the line
Of low, blue, coast that rose before thine eyes
At last, as it had done so oft in sleep,
In those low lengths of sunlit land that stretched
Into the smoking sunset. Thou whose soul
Saw what thine eyes, though fain, were weak to see;
Upon the swift wings of thy dreams, a world
Fast followed and thou didst create the west;
Even as He, the All-Begetting, once,
Sleeping his sleep of the eternities,
Was restless, stirred uneasily in space.
And into being dreamed the universe.

W. Cather
Hesperian, XXII (Nov. 1, 1892), 9.

MY LITTLE BOY

John Esten

I know a wee boy in a far-away land,
    A boy with big eyes of gray,
Who used to fret and hold to my hand,
    And talk to me all the day.

And when all the world went wrong with me,
    And nobody seemed to care,
I'd feel his dear little hand on my knee—
    And my little boy was there!

I meet little fellows wherever I go,
    Some handsomer laddies than he,
You may take, if you want, all the boys that I know,
    But just give my one boy to me.

At the curious tales that I used to tell
    His big eyes would open so wide,
And for fear of the terrible were-wolf's spell
    He used to creep close to my side.

He'd tell the most wonderful romances then,
    That never came out of a book,
Of the rat and the cat and the little red hen,
    And the kitten that fell in the brook.

It was easy to hurt him, this dear little child,
    For he was so gentle and shy,
And if you would laugh when his stories grew wild,
    He always would certainly cry.

If you laughed very hard at what he had said,
    Ah, many the tears he would weep!

He'd run off and creep right under the bed,
    And stay there till he was asleep.

And here in my room, where there is no boy,
    Stands a bed by the empty chair,
Oh, what would I give just now for the joy
    Of finding that little boy there!

Home Monthly, VI (Aug., 1896), 21.

"THINE EYES SO BLUE AND TENDER."

"Thine eyes so blue and tender,"
　　Sang a poet long ago,
Singing of his absent sweetheart—
　　For your eyes he could not know.

Little boy with eyes so trusting,
　　Little boy with cheeks so bright,
Out of all the eyes I've looked in,
　　Only yours come back to-night.

When the loneliness is heavy,
　　And the dark seems coming on,
Your dear eyes look out and tell me
　　That you're sorry I am gone.

Out of all that I have loved so,
　　Of the many and the few,
Is there one of them, I wonder,
　　Who is sorry just like you?

Every sick soul has its comfort,
　　That can make its weakness strong,
Or the cords would snap asunder
　　Sometime, when the strain is long.

Every soul that doubts and wanders,
　　Has its priest who intercedes,
Has its saint who brings God nearer,
　　Mightier than all the creeds.

Little boy, just made for loving,
　　With your laugh so glad and free,
And your eyes so blue and tender—
　　You have done all this for me!

　　　　　　　　Emily Vantell
　　　　　　Home Monthly, VI (Oct., 1896), 15.

JINGLE:

BOBBY SHAFTO

Bobby Shafto fat and fair
Would not comb her yellow hair;
Every morning just at eight
She bewailed her bitter fate.
Then the combs and brush would fly,
All the children going by
Stopped to listen to her cry,
  Pretty Bobby Shafto!

Bobby Shafto fat and fair
Scorned to comb her yellow hair,
But just before she went to school,
She had to sit upon a stool
With her mamma close beside,
While those hateful ringlets dried
And poor Shafto sobbed and cried,
  Pretty Bobby Shafto!

Bobby Shafto fat and fair
Said she'd cut her yellow hair,
But one morning while she cried
Mamma found a mouse inside,
Found a mousie pink and bare,
Who had crept for warmth in there,
Right in Bobby Shafto's hair!
  Pretty Bobby Shafto!

John Esten
Home Monthly, VI (Oct., 1896), 18.

MY HORSEMAN

O, little boy in the West Countree,
    Up with the sun to-day!
Get out your little "trabbling" hat
    With its flowers and ribbons gay.

Get out your yellow Browney horse
    And feed him well with hay,
And brush him down and groom him well,
    You must ride far to-day.

The horse without a mane or tail,
    The horse with legs but three,
Must travel far and travel fast
    To bring you safe to me.

Then rein him up and get the whip,
    The buggy whip will do,
The new one with the cracker that
    The big boys hide from you.

A thousand miles there lies between
    Of wood and waving plain,
And deep ravines where waters rush,
    And rocks washed white with rain.

Soon falls the night on those wide plains,
    And the winds are swift and cold,
But what can fright that gallant steed
    And my dashing horseman bold?

Then never mind the rivers wide,
    Or miles between that be,
But jump upon your steed and ride
    Across the hills to me.

Home Monthly, VI (Nov., 1896), 15.

[THEN BACK TO ANCIENT FRANCE AGAIN]

Then back to ancient France again,
 When Anjou's banner was unfurled.
When life was epic still, and men
 Lived all the love songs of the world.

The Seine divides Old Paris still,
 And half is yours and half is mine;
There, whip in hand, at every inn,
 Spurred chevaliers still quaff their wine.

The old chateau from ruins rise,
 And queens tonight are born anew,
Brought radiant back from shadow land,
 To smile tonight for me and you.

And gallants gay, with powdered hair,
 Shall lead them in the stately dance,
And all those hearts shall beat again,
 Those sad, glad hearts of Olden France!

Lift high the cup of Old Romance,
 And let us drain it to the lees;
Forgotten be the lies of life,
 For these are its realities!

       —W. C.
     Courier, XIV (Apr. 22, 1899), 2.

BRONCHO BILL'S VALEDICTORY

BY WILLA SIBERT CATHER

I've got my walkin' papers,
　　An' I'm goin' to cut my wire,
An' I'll never drink another
　　Till I board the Denver flyer.
I ain't got time for kissin';
　　For I've got a lot to do,—
The fever took me sudden,
　　An' it took no 'count of you.
It took me mighty sudden
　　When I saw a garden wall
With a hedge o' bloomin' sunflowers,
　　An' I knew I'd got my call.
I heard a broncho whinny
　　Down in Central Park to-night,
And a stunnin' woman cut him
　　An' whirled him out o' sight.
He knew me for his brother,
　　Standin' lonesome in the throng,
And the fever took him sudden
　　An' he passed the word along.
I guess I know the feelin'.
　　When it gets a hold that way,
Lord! There ain't enough o' women
　　For to coax a man to stay.
So I've got my walkin' papers,
　　An' I'm goin' to loose the reins,
An' I'll never drink another,
　　Till I strike the Kansas plains.
I'll never take a jack-pot
　　Till I sit and try my luck
Down at Teddy's joint in Denver
　　Where the fellows go to buck;

An' I hear the corks a-poppin';
    An' the beer a-chucklin' low,
An' the billiard balls a clickin',
    With the chaps I used to know,
The ranchers from Wyoming
    An' the fellows from the mines,
A puttin' down the shekels
    An' a puttin' up the wines—
Fellows takin' heavy chances
    Stakin' fortunes on their claim,
An' ridin' down a hundred miles
    To join me in a game.
Chaps who give the dare to fortune
    From the tropics to the snow,
Got their boots in Dawson, maybe,
    An' their hats in Mexico.
Oh! I've got my walkin' papers,
    An' I hate your dirty town,
Where the men'll rob a fellow
    And the women throw him down.
You're not the girl I'm meanin'
    An' you've always done me square,
But you see a man gets restless,
    An' he needs a change o' air.
You can get another sweetheart
    As wears the proper clothes
An' always hunts the tailor
    Where the other chappies goes,
An'll always do you credit
    When he takes you to a ball.
An' is on to all your racket—
    God! I'm tired of it all.
The sunflowers'll be noddin'
    When I strike the cattle land,
An' the sage is gray and dusty
    With the Colorado sand.—
Oh, I'll never drink another
    Till I see the Rockies rise
Big as temples topped on temples

Tipped with snow ag'in the skies;
An' the spires are frozen starlight
    When the day begins to pale—
O! I've got my walkin' papers,
    An' I've got to hit the trail!

Library, I (June 30, 1900), 6.

ARE YOU SLEEPING, LITTLE BROTHER?

TO J. E. C.

Are you sleeping, little brother,
    In the room that once was mine,
Where the night winds sing in summer
    Haunting legends of the Rhine?
Does the aspen by the window
    Whisper still of high desire,
Of the tread of Roman legions
    And the purple pride of Tyre?
On that little iron bedstead,
    Where I've lain so many a night,
Good for vanquished knights, or Caesar
    When the Gauls are put to flight,
Are you sleeping, little brother?

Are you dreaming, little brother,
    Olden dreams that once were mine,
Glorious dreams of kingdom-sacking
    Where the tropic planets shine?
Do those dreams still dwell, I wonder,
    In that little attic room,
Do they steal and take you captive
    To far lands of Orient bloom?
Of the camps toward the sunset,
    Of the warships on the blue,
Of the queens and of the kingdoms
    Waiting, somewhere, just for you
Are you dreaming, little brother?

Are you loving, little brother,
    As another used to do,
Just the rose because it's crimson,
    Just the sky because it's blue?

[73]

Does your heart near burst with loving
    When you hear the larks at morn,
And you see the dew a-glisten
    On the tassels of the corn?
One who never took a kingdom,
    One whose knightly dreams are fled,
One whose coward lance has rusted
    Since his heart was broke and bled,
Could you love him, little brother?

W. S. C.
Library, I (Aug. 4, 1900), 14.

Bibliography

A Note on Editions

Willa Cather's poetry has appeared in four different collections: (1) Willa Sibert Cather, *April Twilights* (Boston: Richard G. Badger, 1903) contained thirty-seven poems, as given in the Table of Contents of the present edition. (2) Willa Cather, *April Twilights and Other Poems* (New York: Alfred A. Knopf, 1923) contained thirty-six poems, twenty-four of them reprinted from the 1903 edition. The thirteen poems omitted from the 1923 and all subsequent editions were "Dedicatory," "Asphodel," "Mills of Montmartre," "On Cydnus," "The Namesake," "White Birch in Wyoming," "Eurydice," "The Night Express," "Thine Advocate," "Sonnet," "From the Valley," "I Have No House for Love to Shelter Him," and "Paris." The twelve new poems added in the 1923 collection were "The Palatine," "The Gaul in the Capitol," "A Likeness," "The Swedish Mother," "Spanish Johnny," "Autumn Melody," "Prairie Spring," "Macon Prairie," "Street in Packingtown," "A Silver Cup," "Recognition," and "Going Home." (3) *April Twilights and Other Poems* was reprinted in 1933, apparently from the same plates, but with one new poem: "Poor Marty" was added at the end to make a total of thirty-seven poems. (4) In the "Library Edition" of Willa Cather's collected works, *April Twilights* is bound in one volume with *Alexander's Bridge* (Boston: Houghton Mifflin Company, 1937). This version of *April Twilights* contains thirty-five poems arranged in two groups, "Early Verses" and "Later Verses." In the first group, two poems that had appeared in all three previous collections were omitted: "In Media Vita" and "Song." The poems in "Later Verses" were the same as in the 1933 edition, but with "Poor Marty" placed next to last and "Going Home" placed last in the volume. In the checklist below, the last three collections are sometimes referred to as the editions of 1923, 1933, and 1937.

A Note on Identifications

The most complete printed bibliography of Willa Cather's poetry has been up to now that by Phyllis Martin Hutchinson in "The Writings of Willa Cather," *Bulletin of the New York Public Library*, LX (June, 1956), 278-281, to which I am much indebted.

In the present listing, unsigned or pseudonymous poems have been identified as Willa Cather's by their subsequent signed publication; by their inclusion in her newspaper columns and articles or in her stories; or by other biographical accounts. John P. Hinz in "Willa Cather in Pittsburgh," *New Colophon* (1950), pp. 198-207, first suggested some of the Cather pseudonyms, among them three used with poems—"Clara Wood Shipman," "John Esten," and "John Charles Asten." The latter two, variations on the name of her brother John Esten Cather, have been completely verified. One new source of identification (which I have studied) is a scrapbook of some of Willa Cather's poems kept by her family. This collection supplies verification of the authorship of poems by "John Esten," "John Charles Asten," "Emily Vantell," "C. W.," and the unsigned poem, "My Horseman." In addition, Willa Cather has initialed or annotated some of the poems in the scrapbook. (See the Appendix for the texts of some of these poems and additional notes.) "Clara Wood Shipman" is a logical pseudonym, as Mr. Hinz points out, but up to now I have been unable to find unassailable proof that all writing with that signature is Willa Cather's.

In the following checklist, Willa Cather's poems are listed chronologically as they appeared in magazines, newspapers, and her own collections. Certain reprints in reviews and books have been included when in context they have some special bibliographical, biographical, or critical interest. Signatures are given for the first appearance of a poem but are omitted for the groups of poems whose first publication was in *April Twilights* of 1903 (Willa Sibert Cather) or *April Twilights and Other Poems* of 1923 (Willa Cather). Sources of attribution for unsigned and pseudonymous poems are indicated by "Scrapbook" (see above), or other notations.

CHECKLIST

OF WILLA CATHER'S POETRY · 1892–1931

1892

 SHAKESPEARE / A FRESHMAN THEME. Signed W. Cather.

  Hesperian, XXI (June 1, 1892), 3.

  James R. Shively, "Willa Cather Juvenilia," *Prairie Schooner*,
   XXII (Spring, 1948), 98-99.

[1892] —— *Writings from Willa Cather's Campus Years* (Lincoln: University of Nebraska Press, 1950), pp. 109-110.

John P. Hinz, "Willa Cather, Undergraduate—Two Poems," *American Literature*, XXI (Mar., 1949), 112-113.

COLUMBUS. Signed W. Cather.

Hesperian, XXII (Nov. 1, 1892), 9.

James R. Shively, "Willa Cather Juvenilia," *Prairie Schooner*, XXII (Spring, 1948), 99-100.

—— *Writings from Willa Cather's Campus Years* (1950),, p. 111.

John P. Hinz, "Willa Cather, Undergraduate—Two Poems," *American Literature*, XXI (Mar., 1949), 114-115.

HORACE / Book I, Ode XXXVIII / "Persicos Odi."

A translation. Signed W. Cather.

Hesperian, XXII (Nov. 24, 1892), 12.

James R. Shively, *Writings from Willa Cather's Campus Years* (1950), p. 112.

1893

[AH LIE ME DEAD IN THE SUNRISE LAND]. With a story, "A Son of the Celestial," signed W. Cather.

Hesperian, XXII (Jan. 15, 1893), 7.

Early Stories of Willa Cather, selected and with a commentary by Mildred R. Bennett (New York: Dodd, Mead & Company, 1957), pp. 25-26.

Willa Cather's Collected Short Fiction, 1892–1912 [edited by Virginia Faulkner], with an Introduction by Mildred R. Bennett (Lincoln: University of Nebraska Press, 1965), p. 523.

1894

ANACREON. Signed W. C.

Sombrero (1894), p. 222.

James R. Shively, *Writings from Willa Cather's Campus Years* (1950), p. 110.

1896

MY LITTLE BOY. Signed John Esten.

[Scrapbook.]

Home Monthly, VI (Aug., 1896), 21.

[1896]

"THINE EYES SO BLUE AND TENDER." Signed Emily Vantell.
[Scrapbook.]
Home Monthly, VI (Oct., 1896), 15.

JINGLE / BOBBY SHAFTO. Signed John Esten.
[Scrapbook.]
Home Monthly, VI (Oct., 1896), 18.

MY HORSEMAN.
[Scrapbook. Inscribed and sent to her brother James Cather.]
Home Monthly, VI (Nov., 1896), 15.

THE THREE HOLY KINGS. A translation from Heine.
[Attributed from accounts by George Seibel and Dorothy
Canfield Fisher. See Introduction.]
Home Monthly, VI (Dec., 1896), 1 and (in part) on cover. Hand-
lettered in a page-illustration by Jane Ames.

1897

THE ERRAND. A translation from Heine. In "The Passing Show,"
signed Willa Cather.
Courier, XII (Nov. 6, 1897), 2.

["HAD YOU BUT SMOTHERED THAT DEVOURING FLAME"]. A translation of three stanzas from Alfred de Musset's "Malibran." In
"The Passing Show," signed Willa Cather.
Courier, XII (Dec. 11, 1897), 2. "My scholarly friends will
laugh at the translation, but I merely wish to get at the
idea."

["THE SEINE DIVIDES OLD PARIS STILL"].
[Stanzas used in 1899 revision, "Then Back to Ancient France
Again."]
Home Monthly, VI (Sept., 1897), 14.

1898

["O! THE WORLD WAS FULL OF THE SUMMER TIME"]. With a story
"The Way of the World," signed Willa Sibert Cather.
Home Monthly, VI (Apr., 1898), 10.

[1898]

> *Courier*, XIV (Aug. 19, 1899), 8.
> *Collected Short Fiction*, p. 395.

1899

["THEN BACK TO ANCIENT FRANCE AGAIN"]. Signed W. C.
> *Courier*, XIV (Apr. 22, 1899), 2. Variant of stanzas 2-4 (unsigned) in *Home Monthly*, VI (Sept., 1897), 14. (See above.)

1900

["IN THAT VOICE WHAT DARKER MAGIC"]. A translation "after Heine." In "The Passing Show," signed Willa Cather.
> *Courier*, XV (Jan. 6, 1900), 2.

IN THE NIGHT. Signed Willa Sibert Cather.
> *Library*, I (Mar. 17, 1900), 16.
> *Courier*, XV (Apr. 7, 1900), 3.

THOU ART THE PEARL. Signed John Charles Asten.
> [Scrapbook. Initialed "W. S. C." by Willa Cather.]
> *Library*, I (Mar. 24, 1900), 16.
> *April Twilights* (1903), and in the editions of 1923, 1933, and 1937.
> *Commonweal*, XIII (Feb. 25, 1931), 465.

"GRANDMITHER, THINK NOT I FORGET." Signed Willa Sibert Cather.
> *Critic*, XXXVI (Apr., 1900), 308.
> Pittsburgh *Leader*, LVI (Mar. 29, 1900), 2.
> *Courier*, XV (Apr. 28, 1900), 2.
> *Current Literature*, XXVIII (May, 1900), 161.
> *April Twilights* (1903), and in the editions of 1923, 1933, and 1937.
> Chicago *Tribune*, May 23, 1903, p. 9. Review.
> *Poet Lore*, XIV (Winter, 1903), 114. Review.
> *McClure's*, XXXII (Apr., 1909), 649.
> *Current Literature*, XLVII (July, 1909), 106.
> *The Home Book of Verse*, edited by Burton E. Stevenson (New York: Henry Holt and Co., 1912), pp. 1015-1016.
> *The Little Book of Modern Verse*, edited by Jessie B. Rittenhouse (Boston: Houghton Mifflin Company, 1913), pp. 75-77.

[1900]

The Answering Voice: One Hundred Love Lyrics by Women,
selected by Sara Teasdale (Boston: Houghton Mifflin
Company, 1917), pp. 108-110.

AFTERMATH (Version 1). Signed Willa Sibert Cather.
Library, I (Apr. 7, 1900), 22.
(See 1903 for Version 2.)

IN THE GARDEN. Signed Willa Sibert Cather.
Library, I (Apr. 14, 1900), 20.

FLEUR DE LIS. Signed Clara Wood Shipman. [?]
Library, I (May 26, 1900), 13.

A LOVE FRAY. Signed Clara Wood Shipman. [?]
Library, I (June 23, 1900), 13.

BRONCHO BILL'S VALEDICTORY. Signed Willa Sibert Cather.
Library, I (June 30, 1900), 6.
Courier, XV (July 14, 1900), 3.

THE LONELY SLEEP. Signed Willa Sibert Cather.
Library, I (July 14, 1900), 18.

ARE YOU SLEEPING, LITTLE BROTHER / To J. E. C. Signed W. S. C.
Library, I (Aug. 4, 1900), 14.
Courier, XV (Aug. 11, 1900), 9. "By Willa Cather."

THE POET TO HIS PUBLIC. [Known later as THE ENCORE.] Signed
Willa Sibert Cather.
Clipping in Scrapbook, unidentified source. ["Christmas"
Lippincott?]
Nebraska State Journal, XXXI (Dec. 16, 1900), 19. A note credits
"Christmas Lippincott, 1900."
April Twilights (1903), and in the editions of 1923, 1933, and
1937, as "The Encore."

ASPHODEL. Signed Willa Sibert Cather.
Critic, XXXVII (Dec., 1900), 565.
Nebraska State Journal, XXXI (Dec. 17, 1900), 4.

[1900]

April Twilights (1903).

The Humbler Poets (Second Series): A Collection of Newspaper and Periodical Verse, 1885–1910, compiled by Wallace and Frances Rice (Chicago: A. C. McClurg and Co., 1911), p. 126.

1901

IN MEDIA VITA. Signed Willa Sibert Cather.

Lippincott's, LXVII (May, 1901), 623.

April Twilights (1903), and in the editions of 1923 and 1933.

WINTER AT DELPHI. Signed Willa Sibert Cather.

Critic, XXXIX (Sept., 1901), 269.

April Twilights (1903), and in the editions of 1923, 1933, and 1937.

New York Times Saturday Review, June 20, 1903, p. 434. Review.

1902

ARCADIAN WINTER. Signed Willa Sibert Cather.

Harper's Weekly, XLVI (Jan. 4, 1902), 24. Unsigned, but "Willa Sibert Cather" is in the list of "Contributors to this number."

High School Journal [Pittsburgh Central High School], VII, no. 4 (Jan., 1902), 1. Signed Willa Sibert Cather.

Courier, XVII (Jan. 18, 1902), 8. "By Willa Sibert Cather."

April Twilights (1903), and in the editions of 1923, 1933, and 1937.

THE NAMESAKE / TO W. L. B. OF THE THIRTY-FIFTH VIRGINIA [or, TO W. S. B. OF THE THIRTY-THIRD VIRGINIA]. Signed Willa Sibert Cather.

Lippincott's, LXIX (Apr., 1902), 482.

Courier, XVII (Apr. 12, 1902), 3.

April Twilights (1903). Subtitle changed to "To W. S. B. of the Thirty-Third Virginia."

THE NIGHT EXPRESS. Signed Willa S. Cather.

Youth's Companion, LXXVI (June 26, 1902), 328.

Nebraska State Journal, XXXII (July 20, 1902), 12.

[1902]

Pittsburgh *Gazette*, Aug. 3, 1902, p. 12.
April Twilights (1903).

IN ROSE TIME. Signed Willa Sibert Cather.
Lippincott's, LXX (July, 1902), 97.
Pittsburgh *Gazette*, July 13, 1902, p. 2.
April Twilights (1903), and in the editions of 1923, 1933, and 1937.
Lincoln *Star*, Oct. 30, 1921, p. 7.
Poetry Review (London), XVI (1925), 408.
Golden Book, V (June, 1927), 723. The last seven lines only are printed.

1903

DEDICATORY.
April Twilights (1903).

MILLS OF MONTMARTRE.
April Twilights (1903).
Academy and Literature (London), LXV (July 18, 1903), 57-58. The first two stanzas only are printed. Review.
Poet Lore, XIV (Winter, 1903), 114-115. Review.

THE HAWTHORN TREE.
April Twilights (1903), and in the editions of 1923, 1933, and 1937.
Poet Lore, XIV (Winter, 1903), 115. Review.
The Answering Voice, selected by Sara Teasdale (1917), p. 34.
Clipping in Scrapbook, unidentified source.
Song, set to music by Jessie L. Pease (New York, 1923).
René Rapin, *Willa Cather* (New York: Robert M. McBride & Co., 1930), p. 15.

SLEEP, MINSTREL, SLEEP.
April Twilights (1903), and in the editions of 1923, 1933, and 1937.

FIDES, SPES.
April Twilights (1903), and in the editions of 1923, 1933, and 1937.
McClure's, XXXII (Feb., 1909), 362.

[1903]

THE TAVERN.

April Twilights (1903), and in the editions of 1923, 1933, and 1937.

New York *Times Saturday Review*, June 20, 1903, p. 434. Review.

McClure's, XXXI (Aug., 1908), 419.

ANTINOUS.

April Twilights (1903), and in the editions of 1923, 1933, and 1937.

PARADOX.

April Twilights (1903), and in the editions of 1923, 1933, and 1937.

PROVENÇAL LEGEND.

April Twilights (1903), and in the editions of 1923, 1933, and 1937.

McClure's, XXXIII (Sept., 1909), 519.

ON CYDNUS.

April Twilights (1903).

Pittsburgh *Gazette*, Apr. 26, 1903, sec. 2, p. 4. Review.

Commonweal, XIII (Feb. 25, 1931), 466.

LAMENT FOR MARSYAS.

April Twilights (1903), and (with the last of the three stanzas omitted) in the editions of 1923, 1933, and 1937.

McClure's, XXX (Feb., 1908), 453.

WHITE BIRCH IN WYOMING.

April Twilights (1903).

I SOUGHT THE WOOD IN WINTER.

April Twilights (1903), and in the editions of 1923, 1933, and 1937.

Golden Book, XIII (Jan., 1931), 70. The third stanza only is printed.

[1903]

Ferris Greenslet, *Under the Bridge* (Boston: Houghton Mifflin Company, 1943), p. 116. Eight lines of the last stanza only are printed.

EVENING SONG.

April Twilights (1903), and in the editions of 1923, 1933, and 1937.

McClure's, XXIX (Aug., 1907), 365. "From 'April Twilights.'"

EURYDICE.

April Twilights (1903).

Commonweal, XIII (Feb. 25, 1931), 465.

THE ENCORE. See "The Poet to His Public," 1900.

LONDON ROSES.

April Twilights (1903), and in the editions of 1923, 1933, and 1937.

McClure's, XXXIV (Nov., 1909), 61.

PRAIRIE DAWN.

April Twilights (1903), and in the editions of 1923, 1933, and 1937.

Dial, XXXV (July 16, 1903), 40-41.

McClure's, XXXI (June, 1908), 229.

Nebraska State Journal, June 10, 1917, p. 3-c.

René Rapin, *Willa Cather* (1930), p. 16.

Commonweal, XIII (Feb. 25, 1931), 466.

David Daiches, *Willa Cather* (Ithaca: Cornell University Press, 1951), p. 177.

AFTERMATH (Version 2).

April Twilights (1903), and in the editions of 1923, 1933, and 1937.

Pittsburgh *Gazette*, Apr. 26, 1903, sec. 2, p. 4. Review.

THINE ADVOCATE.

April Twilights (1903).

[1903]

POPPIES ON LUDLOW CASTLE.
April Twilights (1903), and in the editions of 1923, 1933, and 1937.

SONNET.
April Twilights (1903).
Commonweal, XIII (Feb. 25, 1931), 464.

FROM THE VALLEY.
April Twilights (1903).

I HAVE NO HOUSE FOR LOVE TO SHELTER HIM.
April Twilights (1903).
Poet Lore, XVI (Summer, 1905), 50.

THE POOR MINSTREL.
April Twilights (1903), and in the editions of 1923, 1933, and 1937.
McClure's, XXXVI (Feb., 1911), 376.

PARIS.
April Twilights (1903).

SONG.
April Twilights (1903), and in the editions of 1923 and 1933.

L'ENVOI.
April Twilights (1903), and in the editions of 1923, 1933, and 1937.
The Humbler Poets, compiled by Wallace and Frances Rice (1911), p. 248.
The Home Book of Verse, edited by Burton E. Stevenson (1912), pp. 3217-3218.
Poetry Review (London), XVI (1925), 411.
Commonweal, XIII (Feb. 25, 1931), 465.

1907

AUTUMN MELODY. Signed Willa Sibert Cather.
McClure's, XXX (Nov., 1907), 106.

[1907]

> *April Twilights and Other Poems* (1923), and in the editions of 1933 and 1937.

THE STAR DIAL. Signed Willa Sibert Cather.
> *McClure's*, XXX (Dec., 1907), 202.

1909

THE PALATINE / (IN THE "DARK AGES"). Signed Willa Sibert Cather.
> *McClure's*, XXXIII (June, 1909), 158-159.
> New York *Times Saturday Review*, XIV (May 22, 1909), 317.
> Albert Bigelow Paine, *Mark Twain: A Biography*, III (New York: Harper, 1912), pp. 1501-1502. The first three stanzas only are printed.
> *New Poetry*, edited by Harriet Monroe and Alice Corbin Henderson (New York: The Macmillan Company, 1917), pp. 43-44.
> *April Twilights and Other Poems* (1923), and in the editions of 1933 and 1937.

1911

THE SWEDISH MOTHER / (*Nebraska*). Signed Willa Sibert Cather.
> *McClure's*, XXXVII (Sept., 1911), 541.
> *April Twilights and Other Poems* (1923), and in the editions of 1933 and 1937.

1912

SPANISH JOHNNY. Signed Willa Sibert Cather.
> *McClure's*, XXXIX (June, 1912), 204.
> *New Poetry*, ed. Monroe and Henderson (1917), pp. 44-45.
> *April Twilights and Other Poems* (1923), and in the editions of 1933 and 1937.
> *Literary Digest*, LXXVIII (July 21, 1923), 34.
> *Poetry Review* (London), XVI (1925), 410.
> *American Ballads and Folk Songs*, compiled by John A. and Alan Lomax (New York: The Macmillan Company, 1934). With music by Charles Elbert Scoggins.
> Song, with music by Elmo Russ (New York: U.S. Music, Inc., 1940).
> Song, with music by John Charles Sacco (New York: G. Schirmer, Inc., 1941).

[1912]

Elizabeth Shepley Sergeant, *Willa Cather: A Memoir* (Revised edition; Lincoln: University of Nebraska Press, 1963), pp. 183-184.

PRAIRIE SPRING. Signed Willa Sibert Cather.
McClure's, XL (Dec., 1912), 226.
O Pioneers! (Boston: Houghton Mifflin Company, 1913). Epigraph.
Nebraska State Journal, June 10, 1917, p. 3-c. "From *O Pioneers!*"
April Twilights and Other Poems (1923), and in the editions of 1933 and 1937.
Elizabeth Shepley Sergeant, *Willa Cather: A Memoir* (1953, 1963), pp. 84-85.

1913

A LIKENESS / (PORTRAIT BUST OF AN UNKNOWN, CAPITOL, ROME). Signed Willa Sibert Cather.
Scribner's Magazine, LIV (Dec., 1913), 711-712.
Literary Digest, XLVIII (Jan. 31, 1914), 219.
Nebraska State Journal, Feb. 6, 1914, p. 12.
Anthology of Magazine Verse for 1913, edited by William Stanley Braithwaite (Cambridge, Mass.: W.S.B., 1913), pp. 46-47.
April Twilights and Other Poems (1923), and in the editions of 1933 and 1937.
Poetry Review (London), XVI (1925), 408.

THE DEAD FORERUNNER. Signed C. W.
[Scrapbook.]
Scribner's Magazine, LIV (Dec., 1913), 743.

1915

["ON UPLANDS"]. Dedication to Isabelle McClung.
The Song of the Lark (Boston: Houghton Mifflin Company, 1915).
Elizabeth Shepley Sergeant, *Willa Cather: A Memoir* (1953, 1963), p. 26.
E. K. Brown, *Willa Cather* (New York: Alfred A. Knopf, 1953), p. 97.

[1915]

STREET IN PACKINGTOWN. Signed Willa Sibert Cather.

Century Magazine, XC (May, 1915), 23.

April Twilights and Other Poems (1923), and in the editions of 1933 and 1937.

1923

RECOGNITION.

April Twilights and Other Poems (1923), and in the editions of 1933 and 1937.

MACON PRAIRIE.

April Twilights and Other Poems (1923), and in the editions of 1933 and 1937.

GOING HOME.

April Twilights and Other Poems (1923), and in the editions of 1933 and 1937.

Poetry Review (London), XVI (1925), 409. The last stanza only is printed.

Elizabeth Shepley Sergeant, *Willa Cather: A Memoir* (1953, 1963), p. 24. The third stanza only is printed.

THE GAUL IN THE CAPITOL.

April Twilights and Other Poems (1923), and in the editions of 1933 and 1937.

A SILVER CUP.

April Twilights and Other Poems (1923), and in the editions of 1933 and 1937.

1931

POOR MARTY. Signed Willa Cather.

Atlantic Monthly, CXLVII (May, 1931), 585-587.

Literary Digest, CIX (May 9, 1931), 24.

April Twilights and Other Poems (1933), and in the edition of 1937.